Praise for Flora K. Schildknecht's
MEGAFAUNA

THIS is a fascinating story collection: smart in insight, ferocious about truth, delivered with clarity, steel, and wit. Bad choices, deliberate and otherwise, compose the terrain, and debut author Flora K. Schildknecht explores it with depth and wisdom unusual in an author so young. The dark side of the human heart is in full nuanced display here. It is nothing short of wonderful to see the anger and self-regard of girls and women fully mounted. A breathtaking debut.

—Julie Brickman, *Two Deserts*

MEGAFAUNA is a remarkable collection of short fiction, and one screenplay, exploring the intersection of love and violence, yearning and reversal, signaling the arrival of an exciting voice, evocative and edgy, on the literary scene. In these stories often about young women moving tumultuously from innocence to experience—whether in metropolitan Kentucky or a refugee camp in Calais, France—Flora K. Schildknecht captivates, moves, and unsettles us, reminding us how people struggle to hold each other close as danger lurks around every corner, and often within our own hearts.

—Roy Hoffman, *Come Landfall*

IN her impressive debut collection of stories (and a screenplay!), Flora K. Schildknecht anatomizes humans (and other animals) with all of the precision, intelligence, intuition, and imagination of a scientist and an artist working in close collaboration. In one of the stories, Schildknecht writes about a character's "smile full of teeth that glittered as if she had bitten off pieces of stars from the night sky." The incisive fiction in *Megafauna* has this same, brilliant bite.

—Robin Lippincott, *Blue Territory: A Meditation on the Life and Art of Joan Mitchell*

MEGAFAUNA brims with intelligence and mischief and humor, and with the ravages and unfathomable mysteries of the human heart. In Flora K. Schildknecht's powerfully written and deeply felt debut story collection, her characters often neglect to think the worthy thought or to do the decent thing, but in keeping with their emotional and moral frailties, we are cracked open into a place that demands our own honesty. Reading these stories is like stepping among the strange, beautiful, forgiving shadows found under great, old trees—a sense of our aloneness as human inhabitants on this planet against the backdrop of an ancient desire to connect and belong.

—Eleanor Morse, *White Dog Fell from the Sky*

WITH piercing intelligence and moral candor, the writer of *Megafauna* delivers tales of contemporary life ranging from a migrant camp to a suburban "mommies" club to the wild interior landscape of a child's first inklings of evil. Wayward, devastating, and lyrical, these narratives walk the line between animal and human, bringing us to the precipice of the moral universe and sometimes beyond, as they test what it means to be alive in the twenty-first century. Like Rebecca Lee, the writer unflinchingly explores the trouble we're in, at the same time illuminating new horizons of care and tending, perhaps oneself first of all. A brave new book, every page a revelation.

—Elaine Neil Orr, *Swimming Between Worlds*

THESE stories in Flora K. Schildknecht's debut collection, *Megafauna*, are every one edgy, sly, and delicious, a dark, literary wine with hints of Flannery O'Connor, Lorrie Moore, and Lena Dunham. But it is the author's unmistakable, unique voice that will linger on your palate long after the last savory sentence is downed. Schildknecht uses words in heady ways to construct an immediate, intimate world that is as "lovely and terrifying" as one of her character's smiles. There is nothing ordinary here, these are people you haven't seen, doing things you don't expect—a snake and a child on a stairway, a girl who has inherited only herself, the "raw, violated pink" of sunburn—that are at times subversively hilarious. When the hair on the back of your neck begins to tighten, relax, relish the work; this writer has you safely in hand.

—Lucinda Dixon Sullivan, *It Was the Goodness of the Place*

MEGAFAUNA

MEGAFAUNA

STORIES & SCREENPLAY

FLORA K. SCHILDKNECHT

FLEUR-DE-LIS PRESS 2018
LOUISVILLE, KENTUCKY

Grateful acknowledgement to the following publications in which the following
stories and screenplay first appeared, sometimes in slightly different form: "A
Bad and Sinful Girl" and "Prairie" in *The Louisville Review*; "The Mommies" in *2nd
& Church*; "Bad Signs" in *Sisyphus*; "The Naming of Cats" in *The Chaffin Journal*.

Cover by Matthew Walsh & Jonathan Weinert
Book design by Jonathan Weinert

Printed in the United States of America
First Edition

Library of Congress Cataloging-in-Publication Data
Schildknecht, Flora K.
Megafauna: Stories and Screenplay.
I. Title
Library of Congress Control Number: 2018955337
ISBN 10: 0-9960120-2-8
ISBN 13: 978-0-9960120-2-7

Fleur-de-Lis Press of *The Louisville Review*
Spalding University
851 S. Fourth Street
Louisville, KY 40203
502.873.4398
louisvillereview@spalding.edu
www.louisvillereview.org

I.

II.

III.

For Ron and Hugo

A Bad and Sinful Girl

WHAT EXACTLY IT WAS about Gail that made Maria feel so unsettled she could not say, but looking at the back of Gail's head, Maria wanted to grasp the girl's thin, ash colored pony-tail and give it a good yank—or better yet take the heavy pair of craft scissors she kept in her desk and chop the girl's offen-sively drab, oily gather of hair right off. Maria half listened to their third grade teacher, Mr. Carlson, describe a math prob-lem they were supposed to be solving. *If fifteen of you are buying milk for lunch, and ten are buying juice, how many more students are getting milk instead of juice?* Maria thought about how ugly Gail looked. Maria was convinced that girls should, at the very least, be pretty. Or better, they should be strong. Better still, they should be fierce and mischievous and possessed of all the magic and cunning that would later enable them to rule not only their own destinies, but perhaps even the world. Gail was not pretty and she was certainly not fierce. Pale and almost translucent, her skin was stretched tight over her skinny body. A map of blue veins covered her like a maze of corporeal tributaries. Gail's veins pulsed alarmingly when she was frightened. She was frightened often.

Mr. Carlson called Gail to the front of the class to solve the problem on the board. Gail approached hesitantly, one foot trailing behind the other, as if she were prepared to reverse course at the first sign of danger. But Mr. Carlson was patient and gentle, allowing her to take her time. His excessive kindness infuriated Maria. And how could Gail take so long to do everything? The answer was five. Fifteen minus ten was five. Bored, Maria flipped through her science book, stopping at a picture of a young gazelle, lithe and tawny. She decided that Gail was an inverted version of the gazelle—a stunted, albino, mutant gazelle with thin, colorless hair.

Although Maria knew it was wrong to dislike Gail for being awkward and weak, she could not help it. In Sunday school her teacher, a willowy young woman who was not strong but possessed an irresistibly supple smile, praised the virtues of

4

Gail and her type, saying "blessed are the meek," but this had little practical effect on Maria's feelings of disgust toward Gail. Everything about Sunday school fascinated Maria. Ms. Willow, whose real name was Anne Miller, told almost unbelievable stories about what God wanted and what He could do. He could make a giant whale swallow you whole, just to teach you a lesson. He could cover the whole planet with water if He put his mind to it. He could, according to Ms. Willow, even grant the requests of those who were sincere and prayed every day, which was of great interest to Maria, since there were many things she wanted.

On Friday, Mr. Carlson's students had their once-a-week art class. The quiet, dark boy that Maria usually sat with was absent. Maria and Gail were seated across from each other at the high Formica table and given a box of pastels to share. The art room was located in a basement with no windows, and the air was hot and did not move much. Maria noted Gail was wearing one of her ugliest outfits yet: bright pink corduroy pants with little green hippos on them, topped with a very light pink turtleneck that made her face look pale and unformed. Maria wound a strand of her own thick, dark hair around her finger and sniffed. Her hair still smelled like her mother's shampoo, Pantene. She sniffed the air that hung around Gail. Gail did not smell like Pantene. Gail smelled like urine.

"Listen. These colors here," Maria extracted all the bright and colorful pastels from the box and arranged them on her side of the table, "these are all mine. And if you touch them I'll tell everyone you peed yourself."

"But, we're supposed to share. . . ." Gail looked at the table as she spoke, running her finger across its chipped edge, rubbing some raw color into her bluish fingertips.

"We *are* sharing. All these brown and gray and black ones are yours."

Maria bent over her paper and began to work. She loved art class. Every time she painted or drew something and brought it home, her parents told her how wonderful it was. Surveying the thick, pleasingly pebbled surface of the blank paper, Maria felt a surge of confidence. She sensed that today she would create something truly magnificent.

She decided she would pray as she worked. She prayed she would become an artist so that her parents would buy her art supplies of her very own, so she could practice her craft at home and would never have to share with Gail. If she found herself paired with Gail again, she would just tell the art teacher she had a stomachache and then she would be allowed to lie down in the nurse's office.

Maria drew a picture of her future self. She had thick, abundant hair and a lovely, terrifying smile full of teeth that glittered as if she had bitten off pieces of stars from the night sky. Maria of the future wore a long scarlet dress. Maria of the future was very tall, and she was surrounded by wild animals, drawn to her by her incredible artistic talent. The animals all wanted her to draw pictures of them.

Maria assessed her picture and decided it was her best work yet. There were small flaws; the proportions of the girl's face were somewhat skewed, her smile a little too large. Some of the animals were difficult to recognize without black outlines, but she had given the black pastels to Gail and was not about to ask for them back. Maria was very pleased until she looked over at Gail's drawing.

Using only the dullest colors, Gail had drawn something amazing. It was a portrait of Maria herself in the process of drawing, bent over the table, pastel in hand, a look of intense concentration on her face. The drawing was more like a photograph than any drawing Maria had ever seen. The face was turned just slightly, not looking straight on, not turned all the way to the side, but somewhere between. A thin series of lines represented the side of the face that was turned away. The lines were short dashes when Maria looked at them individually, but when viewed together they made the contour of a cheek, and even an eye, complete with delicate eyelashes. Looking at the image of herself on the page, Maria realized that Gail's drawing was better than hers. The strokes Gail used were minimal and elegant. Maria's lines, which she had originally thought strong, now looked thick and cumbersome. Maria frowned. Gail was smiling, just a little. Maria felt a flush rising across her chest and up her neck, and she wondered if she was turning red.

"Is this supposed to be me?" she said in her most scornful voice, determined to hide the feverish mix of admiration and frustration that was consuming her. Gail stood up and backed away from her drawing, the smile gone, once again looking more like a frightened animal than a girl.

"You don't like it." Gail was now, in effect, talking to the floor. "I'm sorry."

The bell rang and Gail bolted from the room without her drawing, her corduroy pants making fast little *zhoop-zhoop-zhoop* sounds as she went.

At dinner Maria nibbled at her food pensively. It was one of her favorite meals and she felt sure that her parents would notice and ask her what was wrong. She shoved her lasagna this way and that on her plate. She cut off small pieces and placed them on the edge of the dish. It was difficult not to eat much. The lasagna was layered with thinly sliced mushrooms and tender zucchini, and Maria could taste at least two distinctly different cheeses in the small bites she allowed herself. Finally, her parents stopped yammering back and forth about the upcoming election and asked her what was wrong. With a reluctant sigh she'd practiced in the mirror, she explained her problem. She was forced to sit with a smelly, nasty girl in art class who copied her work and hoarded all the black pastels. In spite of this she loved to draw, and she would really like for them to buy her some art supplies because she wanted more than anything to become an artist someday. Her parents looked satisfyingly concerned, and her mother, ever anxious that things should go as Maria wished, pursed her lips and promised to "look into the matter."

Every morning thereafter Maria stared angrily at the back of Gail's head and prayed: *Dear God. Please don't make me sit next to Gail because she is disgusting and steals my ideas. If you do this for me I will be good from now on, I promise.* After three days of this, Gail was absent from class, and Maria thought perhaps her prayers had been answered. But the fourth morning Gail was back again, looking even more weak and disheveled, and sneezing frequently into a dirty tissue she kept tucked in the sleeve of her cheap gray sweater. Just looking at Gail made Maria want to go wash her hands in hot, soapy water.

IN ART CLASS MARIA was relieved to find herself seated across from a girl named Rebecca who smelled like vanilla lotion and was dressed in a freshly pressed denim skirt and a white angora sweater. Rebecca was very pretty, with blue eyes and blonde hair. Rebecca was content to draw brown kitty-cats and red hearts, all of which looked reassuringly childish. She was appropriately impressed by Maria's drawing of the whale that had swallowed the biblical Jonah. Rebecca leaned across the table to admire Maria's clean lines that defined the whale's flippers and tail, making murmurs of appreciation. Maria noticed Rebecca was leaning on her own drawing, and red pastel was being ground into her white sweater. Maria didn't see any reason to mention it.

Halfway through the class Rebecca noticed the big smudge of red on her sweater and began crying inconsolably. She had to be led out of the room to go cry in the hall. Once Rebecca was gone, Maria felt someone staring at her. She heard a wet, sniffling sound, and she turned to see Gail eyeing her from the next table over. There was accusation in her gaze; she obviously thought that Maria had somehow *made* Rebecca soil her sweater and *made* her cry.

When art class was over, Maria saw Gail take her trademark tentative steps toward the art teacher. Ms. Harding was a large, round woman who always wore bright, shapeless dresses with sandals, and her largeness made Gail appear even smaller than usual. Maria had never seen Gail approach a teacher unless called on. She stepped close to Ms. Harding and said something very quietly. The teacher made a point of kneeling down, knees cracking loudly, so she could place her ear closer to Gail's thin bluish lips. Maria wanted to stay and watch. She was sure Gail was telling lies about her, saying it was Maria's fault that pretty Rebecca had ruined her sweater and was now probably sobbing in the nurse's office. Maria would have to set the record straight. She started walking purposefully toward them, but Ms. Harding caught Maria's eye and shook her head firmly. "Maria. Go back to Mr. Carlson's room with your class." Her tone was so dark and full of authority that Maria found herself unable to do anything but obey.

Maria waited for Gail to come back to Mr. Carlson's room. Where could she be? Had Gail told the art teacher about how Maria had taken all the good pastels last week? What had Gail said about Maria ruining Rebecca's sweater? Rebecca herself had calmed considerably; she sat on the other side of the room with her feet primly tucked underneath her in her seat. Rebecca's eyes were puffy but dry, and her sweater had been turned inside out so the stain was not visible.

Finally Gail appeared. She was wearing different pants and looked very sullen. The elastic she always wore in her hair was gone, and her hair hung like a dirty veil across her hunched shoulders. Maria leaned toward her and noticed a smell like an old person's closet—stale and antiseptic.

"Hey, Gail," she whispered. Gail turned around and gave her a wounded look from behind the limp curtain of her hair. Maria sat back in her seat.

Instead of getting on the bus after school Maria followed Gail, who always walked home. As they rounded the corner of the large red brick gymnasium, Maria ran up alongside Gail and shoved her against the wall, hard enough to knock the wind out of her. The girl's exhalation was warm and sour.

"What did you say to Ms. Harding about me?" Maria used the most threatening voice she had. Gail looked frightened, but not as frightened as Maria had hoped.

"Nothing."

Gail's chin quivered and jutted forward, and when she spoke Maria could see that her teeth needed badly to be brushed. She slapped Gail across the face, harder than she had expected to. Gail's eyes squeezed shut and blood oozed from her left nostril. Maria was shocked by the sight of the blood — she had never hit anyone so hard before and had not really wanted to make Gail bleed, but it was too late to back out now. She shook Gail by the shoulders.

"Then what were you talking to her about?"

Gail started to cry in earnest now, snot mixing with the blood dripping from her nose. Maria felt the situation slipping out of her control but gave Gail another good shake anyway.

"I couldn't make it in time," Gail sobbed. Maria slowly realized what was going on. She remembered the way that Gail had smelled before, like pee, and thought about the different pants she had returned to class in, the ones that smelled like storage. She let go of Gail's shoulders, and the girl stumbled away, before breaking into a run, leaving Maria standing alone by the gym with the feeling she had just done something horrible that could never be undone. Maria walked the mile to her own house with the growing feeling that what had just happened proved she was actually, at her core, very, very bad. Gail would tell her parents who would then tell Maria's parents and then everyone would know the truth: she was a wicked, cruel little girl.

The next Sunday was terrible. Ms. Willow was telling the story of the Good Samaritan, but Maria could hardly pay her any attention. She was consumed with fear that Gail would tell someone what she had done. She needed a way to make Gail go away. At the end of the story, Ms. Willow said something interesting. She asked the children to remember her and her husband in their prayers because they were trying to sell their house. She said they had buried a little statue of Saint Joseph in their yard, and they were saying a prayer to him nine times a day, asking him to ask God to help them. This was called intercession.

"Why do you ask the saint when you could just ask God yourself?"

Ms. Willow smiled her placid smile, and it was clear that this was the question she had wanted someone to ask. "We ask the saints to intercede for us because they are especially close to God. They have His ear."

"So why do you bury the statue in the yard?"

Just for a moment Ms. Willow's smile faltered, and Maria could tell this was an unexpected and unwelcome question. Ms. Willow looked as though she did not know how to answer. "It's a tradition." Her gentle smile turned thin and hard for a moment, then she caught herself and gave Maria a knowing, conspiratorial look. "Is there something you want to pray for, Maria?"

Maria said nothing. She had no intention of sharing her plan for personal salvation with Ms. Willow, or anyone else. She feigned shyness and instead offered the Sunday school teacher her most beguiling smile.

"You don't have to tell me. But the most important thing is the prayer. Nine times. Every day. Until your prayers are answered."

During playtime Maria nonchalantly wandered over to the small nativity displayed in the corner of the room. She slipped the small statue of St. Joseph into the pocket of her dress, which fortunately had lots of ruffles that disguised the small, saint-shaped bulge over her left thigh. Maria said a little prayer asking God to forgive her for stealing. She knew stealing was technically bad, but this was for a greater purpose. She knew what she had to do, and why her earlier prayers had not been answered. She'd needed to say them nine times, and she'd needed a statue of St. Joseph.

THE MOON WAS LOW and bright when Maria stepped into the backyard in her nightgown to bury St. Joseph. The grass was dry under her feet and made crisp little sounds as she walked over to the vegetable garden. The tomato plants were fanning out inside their supportive cages, already covered with tiny, whitish-green tomatoes that shone, waxy and pale in the moonlight. She plunged her hands into the soil. Maria had never been outside this late at night alone before. A whispering, crunching sound near the hydrangeas made her pulse quicken, and she stopped digging for a moment. The sound of her own heartbeat throbbed and rushed between her ears. She forced herself to look in the direction of the sound. A small tan rabbit with a white tail munched on clover and regarded her with a quizzical eye. Maria made an encouraging sound and plucked a tomato, offering it to the rabbit, who hopped away. She felt silly for trying to make friends.

St. Joseph looked strange by himself. He was usually positioned next to Mary. The small, bearded man had one arm raised in a meaningless protective gesture. And he wore an expression of earnest adoration as he gazed down at the space where the baby Jesus would normally be.

Maria gave his little plastic face a kiss before putting him in the ground. She added the tomato she had offered the rabbit and scooped dirt into the hole. She made the sign of the cross, touching her fingers to her forehead, belly, and shoulders. She solemnly closed her eyes and whispered her prayer into the quiet night air. The air seemed clearer than the air during the daytime, as if her words might float up to God more easily without all the noise and sunlight in the way.

"Dear Saint Joseph, I need you to ask God to do a favor for me. Please make Gail Wilson go away forever, so she can't tell anyone that I hit her and made her nose bleed." Maria said it eight more times, then added, as she had seen Ms. Willow do, "In Jesus's name, Amen."

Maria made the sign of the cross once more, then walked quickly back to the house. She felt that for the first time in her life she'd said a real prayer, a prayer that had been heard and might be answered. Maria tingled all over with the awareness that she was alive and had just had a secret conversation with a saint.

On Monday Gail's seat was empty. There was no greasy ponytail begging to be cut off, there were no mismatched clothes to ridicule silently. Every time Maria let her eyes trace the contour of the empty chair in front of her, she felt the same rush of excitement she had experienced immediately after she prayed to Saint Joseph. He'd heard her. He'd talked to God about her problem and it had been fixed. The thrill of Gail's removal was almost overshadowed by the realization she had personally communicated, through Joseph, with God. This meant that it was all true, everything they said at church and in the Bible was real, and God was real. Not in some make-believe way but *real* in the same way she was real and school was real and her parents were real. It was a revelation. Maria looked lovingly at Gail's empty desk, proof she lived in a universe where God was real and her wishes could be granted.

For the rest of the week Maria was in a lovely mood. Summer vacation would begin in less than a month, and she was enjoying her days at school so much more now that Gail was out of the picture. At lunch she sat with Rebecca, who always had nice clothes and liked to make lists of the names of boys whom she might someday marry. Rebecca taught Maria how to make little folded paper puzzles that concealed each boy's name under a numbered flap, and they would spend lunch discovering and rediscovering their potential husbands-to-be. There were so many names to think about: Grant, Andrew, Nick, Trevor. The name *Gail* had slipped from Maria's mind.

Rebecca asked if Maria would like to come over to her house on Saturday and see her room. She claimed to have a hundred Barbie dolls. According to Rebecca some of the dolls lived in a big pink house, some had a stable with horses, and some Barbies liked to just hang out by their pool. While Maria doubted anyone could really own that many Barbies, she liked Rebecca and wanted to see her room.

By Friday Maria had all but forgotten about Gail, the conversation with Saint Joseph, and her revelation about the existence of God. But when Mr. Carlson asked for everyone's attention right after they said the Pledge of Allegiance, Maria looked at Gail's empty desk and began to wonder what exactly God had done with her. Resting his hands on the back of Gail's chair, Mr. Carlson told them Gail had developed a rare disease, something called Lymphoma, and she was going to have to stay in a hospital until she got better. When he mentioned "getting better" Mr. Carlson's voice cracked and he began to breathe heavily, and after a moment Maria realized that he was crying, something she had never seen an adult do. Mr. Carlson got hold of himself and explained how Gail had collapsed Monday before class, and she might not return to school at all this year.

Maria felt guilt settle in her stomach like a large cold stone. She trudged through the rest of the day filled with a sense of dread. During art class Maria did not want to draw. She made a series of lines and circles on the page to keep her hands busy, but she really wanted to find a place to hide. She noticed that Rebecca was drawing something other than her usual cats-and-hearts motif and asked her about it. Rebecca seemed bothered that Maria should have to ask what she was drawing, and she explained the picture to her as if Maria were very slow. "Here's Gail in bed at the hospital." Rebecca gestured to a stick figure lying prostrate on a lopsided blue square. "And these are the angels waiting to take her up to heaven." The angels Rebecca pointed to were misshapen and awkward, but nonetheless looked ready to carry Gail up and out of the bed.

Maria knew her friend was a simple girl who sometimes misunderstood the things adults said, so she gently corrected her. "Mr. Carlson didn't say that Gail was going to *die*. She's only going to be in the hospital until she gets better." Maria realized as she spoke how unlikely this sounded.

Rebecca just looked at her and began coloring the angels' wings a deep blue.

When they got back to their classroom Gail's desk was gone, and Grant and Sophie's desks, which had been on either side of Gail, had been pushed together.

As soon as she got home, Maria slipped into her backyard and walked briskly over to where she had buried St. Joseph, right in the middle of the garden between the second and third tomato plants. But where he should have been there was just a hole, and next to the hole was the rabbit-chewed nub of what used to be a tomato. Maria sat down in the dirt and looked under the plants for St. Joseph. She looked under the hydrangea bush and along the line of the fence, but he was not there.

Maria went inside and flung herself on her bed. She prayed to God—not just nine but ninety times—not to make Gail die. She told God that all she had wanted was for Gail to go away, not to heaven but to someplace far off but nice sounding. Like California.

Rebecca's mother called the next day to see when Maria was coming over. Maria told her parents she was not feeling well and wanted to stay home.

Maria prayed every day for Gail to return to class unharmed, but Gail did not return and Mr. Carlson never mentioned her. Rebecca stopped talking to Maria. Maria guessed she was angry with her for not coming to see her collection of Barbies, but she did not care. The inside of Maria's head was draped with the dark knowledge of what she had done.

"WHEN ADAM AND EVE chose to eat from the Tree of Knowledge, they lost their innocence and became sinners." On Sunday Ms. Willow's voice was serene, and she wore a long, rose-colored skirt that swished, petal-like, past Maria and the other children seated on the floor in front of her.

"We call this *Original Sin,* and it is passed down to all of us, inherited, like a last name. We are *all* sinners, from birth." Maria absorbed this knowledge with numb terror. She had somehow known it all along, that she was bad, that a seed of sin existed deep within her. If she looked past the pink folds of Ms. Willow's skirt, Maria could see the empty place in the Sunday school's nativity where St. Joseph had been.

Ms. Willow caught her eye and seemed to be speaking directly to her. "Everyone sins. It is a sin to disobey your parents. It is a sin to be mean to other children. Stealing is a sin. It is a sin to think bad thoughts. You know when you have committed a sin because it separates your heart from God, and you feel bad."

After Sunday school Maria's parents said they had a surprise for her. Waiting in the backseat of their car was a heavy package, wrapped in glittery paper. Maria tore at the paper halfheartedly, knowledge of her own sinful nature making her nauseous. The package contained a deluxe set of oil pastels and a tablet of heavy drawing paper. Maria tried to look happy for her parents' sake, but she tumbled deeper and deeper down the hole inside her own heart, imagining the space between her and God growing larger and more black by the minute. She was beyond saving. She had prayed for her own art supplies and now she had them. She had prayed for Gail to go away, and now Gail was dead. On the drive home she took out one of the dark purple pastels and ground some of it into the beige carpeting on the floorboard of her parents' car. Maria knew it was bad, and she knew she would probably be punished when her mother or father noticed the stain. She couldn't help herself. She was by nature a bad and sinful girl.

DANGER ON THE STAIRS

DRIVING UP THE GRAVEL strip to the dirty-looking white prefab Sonja shared with Craig and the girls, I knew it was a mistake to come. But, I needed a model. I needed a little girl, and Sonja was the only person I knew who had a young daughter and would allow her to be photographed for my art project. The yard was a forbidding jungle of discarded children's toys and metal animals welded together out of garden tools. Craig welded for an outfit called *Yard Beasts*, fabricating scrap metal and oversize nuts and bolts into yard ornaments, and he was allowed to take the factory seconds home, as a bonus. On either side of the stoop a pair of creatures, *birds? dinosaurs?* seemed to leer at me, extending sharp, garden rake hands in my direction.

I knocked softly on Sonja's thin metal door, and the dogs started banging around inside and barking like mad. Sonja always had dogs. When we were in high school together she had a new dog almost every month. Sonja would find a dog, fall in love for a few weeks, only to drop it off on the outskirts of town when things didn't pan out between them. *She wouldn't listen*, she would say. *He chewed up my favorite bra*, she would say. *She was a bitch*, she would say and shrug, then never mention that dog again.

"Hurry up goddamn it," Sonja yelled at someone. I heard several yelps, then claws scraping against the walls. A door slammed shut, and the barking continued vehemently, but now muffled, as if from some more enclosed recess. Melissa opened the door with nothing on but a too-big Nascar T-shirt. Half her long blonde hair was chopped off so it hung just a few inches above her shoulders. The hair on the other side was so long it almost touched her waist. She was smiling.

"Mommy did my hair."

Sonja strode into view behind her daughter, smoking a long thin cigarette. Even after three babies, she exuded the same striking, hungry, Eastern European beauty she had when I met her in the ninth grade. Sonja had been adopted from Ukraine when she was ten years old. People in our old neighborhood said she never fit in, never looked or acted like she belonged in Kentucky. In some ways she had assimilated. Instead of the black miniskirt and tight black T-shirt she always wore to high school, she was dressed in stonewashed jeans and a pink halter-top. The clothes could have belonged to any young mother living in the mobile home parks here in the south end of Lexington. But her face—and the eyes—still somehow indicated that she was not from here and never would be.

"You better come in. Missy here is taking forever to get ready." Sonja gave the long side of the girl's hair a little yank and turned into the darkness of the house. I followed her. Sonja stubbed out the cigarette in the overflowing ashtray, flopped down on the ripped pleather sofa, and started twisting up a joint.

"For later," she explained. I didn't bother telling her that I had stopped smoking pot years ago, and that she probably should, too. After all, we were both adults now, twenty-six years old. The dogs whimpered and scratched from behind the bedroom door. Sonja seemed not to notice. I stood in Sonja's dirty living room, between heaped laundry and stacks of magazines, feeling very out of place in my outfit. Instead of my usual tight jeans and baggy T-shirt ensemble, I had paired a medium brown sweater with a slightly darker brown pencil skirt and a pair of brown suede kitten-heel pumps, thinking it would make me look scholarly, maybe even a little intimidating. But now I just felt like a fool—as if I thought that brown was the color of professionalism. It might have worked if I had chosen black.

When I met Sonja, she had already lived in the States for a few years, but she still spoke with a Russian-sounding accent. Her adoptive parents, Eileen and Bob Beasley, were devout Baptists who never had any children and wanted a little girl of their own. They lived close enough that I had heard about her adoption, but far enough so that I never met Sonja until she and I were in homeroom together at Taylor High School. I had heard from my mother that the Beasleys wanted to adopt a baby, but instead the agency offered them ten-year-old Sonja, and gave them the hard sell—told them that Sonja had been in the orphanage for most of her life and she would be put out on the street when she turned thirteen if no one adopted her. Bad things would probably happen to her out there, things good Christians like the Beasleys would not stand for.

Chewing on a strand of her dark hair in homeroom, Sonja had looked like one of the Russian mail order brides my older brother Benny was always ogling on the "dating" websites— thin and edgy and with crooked teeth and huge dark eyes.

She asked me to help her get some Marlboros. She called all cigarettes Marlboros. She wore lipstick and a black lace bra that pushed up her small breasts so they curved over the top of her low-cut shirt. Her clothes were always tight and short and black. Sonja was the kind of girl my own parents thought would get me mixed up with the wrong crowd. I told them she didn't run with any crowd. They didn't believe me.

For the first two years of high school, I was fascinated with her. She was the only girl I had met who didn't need anyone's approval. I always felt that she was just allowing me to hang out with her, and that she really wouldn't have cared if she were with me or with someone else. I loved watching her smoke. I loved the way she'd throw her lipstick-stained cigarette butts on the pavement of the school parking lot and then smile, almost sweetly, as if to say, *so what?*

Halfway through junior year she had the first baby, Harriet, and moved in with Craig and his parents. And then I mostly forgot about her. We talked on the phone a few times a year. After Harriet there was another little girl, Riley, and then a few years later Melissa was born. After that Sonja swore she wasn't going to have any more kids, unless she could make sure she would have a boy—for Craig. She said they already had more girls than they knew what to do with. We met for coffee occasionally and smoked joints in my car. I promised I would visit, play with the girls, but I never did. I hadn't seen Sonja since before I started college, almost four years ago, and I might not have ever called her if I hadn't needed to use Melissa for a model. I was there because I needed something, and we both knew it. I paced and Sonja sat on the sofa; she looked as bored and defiant and sexy as ever.

"What's with her hair?" I asked. Sonja shrugged.

"She gave her doll a haircut like that. I wanted them to match." Sonja said. "It's not going to mess things up for you, is it? For your photo shoot?"

"I can just turn her to the side," I said. "Did you tell her about the snake?"

Sonja lit up a fresh cigarette.

"Yeah. I told her."

Melissa came out of her bedroom. She was wearing a lot of pink lipstick and was dressed in an outfit that looked like a miniature version of Sonja's: too-tight stonewashed jeans, and a pink T-shirt that said *Princess* in glittery bubble letters.

"I'm ready for my glamour shot!" Melissa said. Sonja waved us off, and I waited for a minute, sure Melissa would want to say goodbye to her mother, or that Sonja would demand a kiss or a hug, but Sonja said nothing, so we left.

•

MY ASSIGNMENT WAS to make a photograph inspired by a classic painting, but, my instructor had said, her eyes gleaming, *with a twist*. My senior college advisor said that even a General Studies major had to have at least one art elective. Photography sounded easy. You point the camera at something, push the button, and that's it, you're done. I liked the photographs of Nan Goldin, especially the ones where everyone was high and drunk and screwing one another. I liked less the ones where they were sick with AIDS, but it had been the eighties and that was what was going on then. I looked through the books of classical paintings at the school library and decided that they were all completely boring. I couldn't make any photographs based on blurry water lilies, or rich people having lunch or going to the opera or the ballet or whatever else they did. Finally, I found a painting of a large boa constrictor sliding down someone's ornate staircase. *Danger on the Stairs*, it was called, by Jacques-something-or-other, a French guy. I knew someone with a large snake. And I had a big staircase I could use right in my apartment building. It was just a plain, concrete and metal staircase, but I knew that didn't matter. I could tell the instructor I was reinterpreting the painting—she'd love it. I just needed the so-called twist on the photograph.

I was the only non-art major in the class, and everyone else was deadly serious about photography. All the students looked years younger than me. I had started college later than them, since after high school I spent three years working at the coffee shop Sonja and I had always gone to. At first I'd intended just to take a year off, take a break from school. But one year turned into three, and my parents were begging me to move out, go to college, to start doing something. I'd like to say this span of time was filled with something meaningful: a long, tumultuous relationship with a first love that ended in a climactic breakup that left me emotionally devastated, or a series of casual encounters with guys whose names I would not remember after a few months. Instead, there was Stan. I had known Stan since grade school. Occasionally there was sex, but mostly out of boredom. Sometimes, we went to the movies.

The photography students were always bringing in photos of old people and children. My photography instructor, a woman with a thin nose and a nervous, birdlike way of moving, always praised these photos, saying that the kids and old folks gave the work "depth." I decided that to have depth in my photo I should place a child on the stairs with the snake. I would make sure that the child had all the visual cues of innocence. The concept of visual cues was the only useful thing that I felt I had learned in photography class—visual cues were all about manipulating how people perceived things by understanding stereotypes. What could be more innocent, I thought, than a little girl, dressed in one of those plaid Catholic schoolgirl uniforms? So I had called Sonja and asked if I could borrow Melissa for an afternoon. When Sonja said yes, I found out Melissa's dress size and went directly to the discount school uniform store I had noticed on the drive between my apartment and the university. Buying the uniform had been an unnerving experience. The friendly clerk, who looked like a Norman Rockwell granny, assumed that I was shopping for my own daughter.

"Where is your daughter starting school?" Granny Rockwell asked.

"St. Raphael," I said. There was a St. Raphael in my old neighborhood.

"Is she starting kindergarten or first grade?"

"Kindergarten."

"Oh! Then she'll need the jumper instead of the skirt set. Those are for the first graders and up." Granny was back at the rack in a second, getting an impossibly starchy little jumper with a gold cross embroidered on the left breast pocket.

"Of course. I forgot. Thanks."

•

I'D ALWAYS ENVIED the way that everyone in school looked at Sonja. I loved that she made my parents nervous. I'd always been jealous of the way she seemed not to care what anyone thought. And now I had her youngest daughter in my car, drumming her hands on the dash to a Lady Gaga song on the radio, looking like a tiny version of her mother. I was going to take her picture with a huge snake that my neighbor was going to bring over. The snake was currently relaxing in a large cooler with ice packs, to make it less mobile and easier to position. After I took the picture, I was going to return Melissa to her mother, and they would live in the little white house with the tacky lawn sculptures until Melissa grew up and escaped, or had a baby of her own, whichever came first. I would pass my photography class and graduate and get a good job, and never think of them again. That was the plan. Melissa gave me a smile that looked just like the way Sonja used to smile when we were friends; Melissa asked me if we could stop and get her a haircut.

"I don't really like it," she said, running her fingers through the short side of her hair. "I just don't want to hurt Mommy's feelings. We can say you made me do it. For the photo."

"Okay," I said. I drove for a few blocks, past several strip malls. Lexington is full of strip malls. I pulled over at a Great Clips. Melissa bounded out of the car and through the doors of the salon before I even had the engine off. By the time I got in behind her, she had already set things in motion. I was greeted by a heavy woman with a nametag that said Wanda.

"Your daughter said she needs a haircut," Wanda said. Melissa was already in the chair.

"That's right," I said. "She cut her hair to look like her doll's. She needs it evened out."

"Thanks, *Mom,*" Melissa beamed.

With a few minutes of snipping, Wanda had Melissa's hair all evened out. But Melissa wasn't satisfied. "Can you give me bangs, like Mom has?"

I had recently gotten bangs in an attempt to update my image, and I hated them. Unless I turned them under with a curling iron, as I had this morning, they stuck out every which way and looked ridiculous. It was too much work. Would Sonja care about keeping Melissa's bangs looking neat? Would Melissa just wind up looking even more disheveled? Wanda was waiting for my approval. Melissa wriggled impatiently in the chair, silently begging me to let her have her way.

"Sure," I said, "why not."

•

Melissa loved my tiny apartment. The furniture was all secondhand or IKEA, but she asked about every little thing, like she had never seen a set of bath towels that matched the shower curtain and bath mat. I helped her get into the schoolgirl uniform. It fit perfectly. I left the sales tags attached and carefully taped them to the inside of the garments so I could return the outfit after the photo shoot. We stood in my bedroom in front of a floor-length mirror that I used primarily to stare at my own reflection disapprovingly. (I had progressed from the high school stage of worrying if my boobs were big enough to the college stage of worrying that they were *too* big, and made me look fat.) She was blonde and I had hair that was light brown, but our haircuts matched. My frumpy outfit somehow fit with her school uniform, and we looked like we belonged together, almost like she could be my daughter. Maybe I would've been a better mother than Sonja. Would I be a more capable parent, just because I didn't leave full ashtrays around and bought matching bath sets? Probably not, but it was nice to think, just for a minute, that I might at least make a better *looking* parent than Sonja.

Melissa couldn't believe that I had a bedroom all to myself.

She shared her room with the older girls. I asked how the girls were doing. "Riley lets me wear all her old clothes. But Harry's mean. She locks me out. And she smokes." She pretended to take a drag off an imaginary cigarette. I guessed the oldest girl had decided *Harriet* was too old-fashioned and was going by *Harry*.

"Last time she locked me out all day long, and I had to pee in the yard."

Before I could ask where her parents had been during the day Melissa had been locked outside, or why they were letting eleven-year-old Harriet smoke, there was a loud knock at the door, and I went to greet the neighbor who was there with the snake.

The neighbor, Rick, was standing outside the door with a very large, battered cooler. It was hard to tell Rick's age, but he looked somewhere close to forty. He had a lazy eye and long, stringy, red hair. He peered over my shoulder at the inside of my apartment like he was casing the place. I had always been uneasy around Rick, ever since he cornered me the day I moved in and wanted to show me his snakes. He looked like the kind of man that one might warn their children not to get too close to, and I disliked the idea of him being around Melissa. But I disliked more the idea of being alone with the snake.

"She's good and relaxed. She just ate this morning." Rick flipped open the cooler lid where the snake, a boa that had to be at least six feet long, lay draped over several ice packs. He traced a large bulge in its midsection with a finger with a lot of dirt under the ragged nail. "Grade-A lab rat," he said, lovingly. I asked Rick to wait on the staircase with the snake while I got Melissa and my camera.

MELISSA HAD NOT BEEN told about the snake. She sat on the step in the starchy jumper, trying not to cry and not quite succeeding. Rick draped the snake along the metal banister beside her. I stood back with the camera, a heavy, almost antique thing that used real film, and tried to frame the shot. It didn't look good. Even with her new haircut, Melissa did not look convincingly like a Catholic schoolgirl. Her sneakers were pink and dirty, and they looked out of place with the plaid uniform. I hadn't thought to supply her with those shiny black patent shoes that schoolgirls surely wore.

"Take your shoes off, Melissa," I said.

Melissa sniffed, but she did as she was told. Thankfully, she was wearing socks that were clean and white. One sock scrunched down and the other was pulled up high, giving her a disheveled appearance. I thought it looked charming, like she was just getting ready for school and didn't have her shoes on yet.

I couldn't seem to find an angle that showed Melissa and the snake without having Rick in the picture, too. He was keeping one hand on the snake to make sure it didn't escape. But the snake looked fairly docile. "Rick, could you let go of her for just a minute?" Melissa's eyes got huge.

"Don't worry, honey," Rick said. "She's ain't goin' nowhere. She ate earlier today, and all she wants to do right now is relax and work through breakfast." Rick took his hand off the snake and moved a few steps away. The snake lazily lifted its head from the banister and turned toward Melissa. Its dark tongue flicked the air. The snake started moving slowly in Melissa's direction. Melissa began to sob quietly and shrunk down on the stairs. I started snapping off as many shots as I could. Rick started to step in and retrieve the snake, but I motioned him to stay where he was. "Don't move!" I said to him, sternly.

The snake was sliding down the stairs now, right past Melissa's feet in the little white socks. She was staying completely still and squeezing her eyes shut. I shot every angle I could think of as the snake slowly moved past Melissa. It was all over in a few minutes. Rick picked up the snake from the foot of the stairs and put her proudly back in the cooler. "She did great, didn't she?"

ON THE RIDE HOME Melissa was sullen. She refused my offer to stop at Dairy Queen, which I would have thought no child could resist. She was still wearing the schoolgirl uniform; when I wasn't looking she had removed the tags from the outfit, so now it couldn't be returned. Her new bangs were starting to frizz out awkwardly; they would need to be smoothed down with a curling iron soon. Surely Sonja had a curling iron.

We pulled up in front of Sonja's house. The sun was going down, and in the fading light Craig's metal yard animals looked even more fierce and intimidating, casting long, purple shadows on the gravel drive. There were no lights on inside, and no cars in the driveway. I got out of the car, walked up to the door and knocked. Nothing. I dialed Sonja's number on my cell phone, and I heard the phone inside the house ring through the flimsy door. No dogs barked. I walked back to my car and got in. Melissa was still sitting in the passenger seat.

"Nobody's here," I said. Sonja was probably just out getting groceries or something like that. "Does your mom usually take the dogs with her when she goes out?" Melissa said nothing. "What time does your dad get home?"

Melissa smoothed her skirt and folded her hands in her lap. "He left," she said, her voice small.

"When?" I asked.

"Last week. Riley and Harriet left with him. He said he'd come back for me. He said he'd come back and take the dogs, too." There was a long silence while I tried to think of something to say.

"I'm sure he'll be back," I said, finally. Melissa looked doubtful. "I'm sure Sonja will come home," I said, but I was not sure at all.

We waited in the driveway for an hour, and the sun went the rest of the way down. It got cold. I could call Sonja's adoptive parents, the Beasleys, and tell them that Sonja had run away, and left Melissa behind. I wondered if they still lived down the street from my parents. The Beasleys could keep her for a while and track down either Craig or Sonja. Or maybe both parents were gone for good, and the grandparents would raise the girl from now on. Melissa was nodding off in the seat next to me.

"Hey," I said. "I have a great idea. You can spend the night at my place tonight."

"Like a sleepover?" Melissa asked.

"Exactly. We'll have a sleepover." She loved that idea.

AT MY APARTMENT I made a frozen pizza. Melissa ate most of it. I had forgotten that children need to eat almost all the time—I mostly lived on bananas, granola bars, and coffee. After the pizza, I got out a pint of double fudge chocolate ice cream, gave Melissa a spoon, and let her eat it right from the container.

"I bet Mommy wishes she was here right now, spending the night at your house," she said, between bites of ice cream.

"Really?" I asked, only half listening. I was already starting to doubt the wisdom of my sleepover idea. Shouldn't I be calling someone—the Beasleys, the police? What if Craig was prowling around Lexington, looking for his daughter?

"Mommy says in high school, you were her best friend," she said, running her finger around the rim of the nearly empty paperboard ice cream container. This seemed unlikely, I thought. Sonja never said things like that.

After letting her binge on ice cream, I decided I should fix Melissa's newly cut bangs with the curling iron. By now they looked just as frizzy and wild as mine did. I knew it was a silly thing to do right before putting her to bed, but I wanted to do it anyway. She held so still as I smoothed her bangs that it seemed as if she had stopped breathing. I gave her one of my old T-shirts to sleep in. I found a spare toothbrush and told her to brush her teeth. She complained, but only a little. I put her in my bed and when I came back to check on her a few minutes later, she was already asleep. In the dark, her profile looked just like her mother's.

I got comfortable on the sofa and tried to decide what I would do with Melissa in the morning. Once, Sonja had run away from the Beasleys. I hid her in our garage for three days before our parents caught on. During the third day that Sonja was "missing," I cut school and spent all afternoon with her, lounging in the hammock in my parents' backyard. The ropes pressed thick red marks into our thighs, and we talked about where we would escape to when we grew up—Hollywood, New York, or just out West. We always talked about escaping. When Sonja was discovered, the Beasleys weren't angry with her; in fact, they let her do almost anything she wanted from that point on.

I woke Melissa up a little before dawn. She was soft and cooperative, like her mind was fuzzy around the edges. We got into my car quietly, like thieves, like spies, like criminals. We took I-64 out of town, heading west toward Louisville. We

were safely out of Lexington by the time the sun was up. I noticed Melissa had traced our names in the condensation on her
window with her fingertip.

"Are we running away?" she asked.

"Would you like to go to the zoo?" I said.

"Yes."

My cellphone buzzed, Sonja's number on the caller ID. I
silenced it and stuffed it as far down in my bag as possible. I
wondered how hard it would be to change our names, how far
we would have to travel from Sonja and Craig and her family
to be safe. We would probably need to leave Kentucky behind
if we really wanted to escape.

The zoo in Louisville was not as thrilling as I had hoped.
As soon as we entered the park there was a large pit with an
artificial hill in the center of it. The inhabitants of the mound
of plastic contoured to look like a pile of boulders appeared
to be only a few listless brown monkeys with matted fur and
a nasty, pungent smell that stung our eyes. Melissa asked if
I thought the monkeys were happy. I told her I thought they
were usually fine, but that today they were probably too hot.
She rolled her eyes at me and said, "Whatever." The lions,
which Melissa had chattered about seeing all morning, refused
to show themselves. She swore she could make out the shape

of one of the big cats in one of the shadowed corners of the habitat, and she insisted we stand in front of the exhibit for almost an hour, squinting across the moat in the afternoon heat. I finally told her it was time to leave when I realized that she was getting sunburned—the fair skin on her nose and shoulders had turned an angry shade of red. As we walked toward the exit we passed a building called the Herpaquarium. The gray sheet metal structure was painted, badly, with a mural of a rainforest. A banner across the front door read *Reptiles of the Amazon* in snakeskin patterned letters.

"What's in there?" she asked.

"Oh, just reptiles," I said.

"You mean, like, snakes?"

"Yeah."

She scowled at me, narrowing her eyes, and I pretended not to notice. We walked back to the car in silence, and I remembered that when we were in school, Sonja had had a gift for ignoring me when she was angry. Sometimes she had refused to speak to me for weeks at a time.

I got us a room at a Motel 6 that had looked nice from the outside but had peeling wallpaper and a frightening amount of mildew in the bathroom. I had stuffed the trunk of my car with essential items, including the curling iron, but Melissa did not want me to fix her hair.

"It looks silly," she said. "I shouldn't have cut it." She sulked the rest of the night, only eating a few bites of the General Tso's chicken and beef lo mein I ordered, declaring that Chinese food was "weird." Her bangs frizzed. Her sunburn blistered. That night, she wet the bed and woke crying, demanding that I take her home. After I finally got her back to sleep, I stepped outside the room and called Sonja. Her phone went to voicemail. I left a long, rambling message, explaining that when we couldn't find her, I decided to take Melissa on a short road trip to pass the time, but even as I was speaking I could tell I sounded crazy. I promised we'd be back in town tomorrow morning.

When we got back to Lexington the next day, Sonja was waiting at my apartment building, with an especially large, black dog in tow. She had its leash in one hand and one of her skinny cigarettes in the other, smoldering. The monstrous dog keened and drooled at the sight of Melissa, straining the leash. The dog was a mutt and appeared to have inherited the most menacing traits of the German Shepard, the Rottweiler, and the wolf of my bad dreams. I hated big dogs. Melissa squealed with delight and ran over to the thing, throwing her arms around it. Sonja said nothing. She just glared at me, with a look of malice that was exceptional, even for her. She tossed her lit cigarette on the steps of my apartment. She opened the door to her crappy little white two-door car, and the three of them got in and drove away.

I KEPT ONLY ONE of the photographs I took of Melissa. Her feet, planted on the stairs, in those cottony white socks, one pulled up and the other slouching, the glistening body of the snake sliding by in the foreground. The hem of her plaid schoolgirl uniform, almost covering her knees. There is a dark bruise on her shin that I failed to notice at the time. My teacher said it was a great visual cue, that bruise, but she never said of what.

ARITHMETIC

WHEN ROSE AND I rode our bikes to my father's house and saw him sitting on the steps in those sad, worn pajamas, holding himself like that, I almost decided not to go to him at all. But he'd phoned me for help. And since Rose didn't take classes on Fridays and I wasn't actually required to be on campus outside of office hours, we'd headed over. He hadn't seen us riding by yet, and I considered not stopping at all, just coasting away before he noticed us.

"What are you doing, Amy?" hissed Rose. I didn't say anything. Rose had never met my father before, and she wouldn't understand my hesitation, my instinct to keep pedaling before he saw us. And it wasn't really a question, anyway. She was already turning around, and in a moment she was tossing her bike into the thorn grass in his yard and running over to him.

"Mr. Swanson," she called. He stood, unsteadily. His face was a mess of blood and bruises. She let out a breathy little gasp that sounded slightly rehearsed when she saw the face. And what had she expected, I thought, already angry with her for inserting herself into the situation. He had practically collapsed on top of her and she was swaying under his weight. Together, we helped him stagger into his house.

It was dark inside. The tall windows were covered by heavy velvet drapes in a maudlin shade of burgundy. Furnished differently, the house would have been a gracious, if aging, New Orleans beauty, but every room was thick with his awful paintings and drawings, all in various stages of completion. The smallest were the size of a postcard, the larger ones spanned the entire side of a room and almost touched the fourteen-foot ceilings. The bentwood chair that had belonged to his mother lay overturned, one of its delicate legs cracked in half. A smear of something dark and viscous stained the knotty pine floor. I tried to tell myself it was probably oil paint. Nearby a pair of ripped jeans, soiled with the same ruddy substance, lay crumpled like a wounded animal. There were no other signs of the robbery he had spoken of when he called me an hour ago.

The place stank. Like many residents of the Ninth Ward, my father had refused to install air conditioning, and the ever-present heat was fermenting the contents of the house. A swampy, ripe perfume hung in the air that had notes of rotting fruit, linseed oil, and stale beer. Wherever his paintings were not displayed, he had hung what he called his found objects. Junk, really, mostly rusty pieces of old cars he had scavenged. A lone headlight dangled by its wires from the ceiling fan like a disembodied eye, swaying slowly back and forth as the fan turned. I remembered coming to the house when it belonged to my grandmother. It had been full of light and decorated with tasteful antiques. She would have hated what he'd done with the place.

Rose stood in front of a massive canvas that depicted a seaside at dawn. Sitting on the beach with her face turned away was a giant nude woman, towering over the dunes. She was young, about Rose's age, with a heavy, curving shape and white skin that reflected the pink and violet hues of the sunrise. Her back was a layered mass of scars, like she'd been whipped repeatedly. It was a typical example of his work—he often used the same crude formula: stunning landscape, naked woman, evidence of violence. It was beyond foolish, I thought, as if *this* plus *that* automatically equaled something meaningful, arithmetic masquerading as art. In the real world, things had to make more sense than that, which was why I believed science would kick art's ass any day of the week.

Rose stared, mesmerized by the huge painting. I'd been afraid she would fall in love with his work. An undergraduate art student, Rose had the notion that making something big meant making something good. Her area of interest was textiles, and last year her thesis project was an upholstered hamburger the size of a sofa. Lately she'd been filling our side of the duplex with giant food made of cloth. When I came home yesterday, a five-foot-wide sunny-side up egg was hanging on the wall behind the sofa.

"Aren't you going to call the police, and report the robbery?" I asked, and Rose finally stopped staring at the painting.

"The police. What could they do, anyway? File a report?" He spoke from where he'd settled across the room in the shadows. His voice was quiet and resigned, and he sat hunched over on a stool as if he were trying to take up the least amount of space possible. I approached him and realized the stale beer odor was actually emanating from his body, rather than the house.

"What did they take?" Rose asked, looking at the wounded pants on the floor with suspicion.

"Not much. But I think they broke my nose." He covered his face with his hands, as if he did not want us to look at him.

"You need to go to the hospital," said Rose, decisively.

And so we went, leaving the bikes on the lawn and Ubering over to University Hospital with him squeezed between us, reeking. En route, Rose insisted that he would be staying at our place, until he got better. Our place. Just hearing her say it like that, so casual and so full of authority, made me queasy. Of course I wanted her to think of the house as ours, but I didn't want her inviting my father in. It was a terrible idea.

The young Hispanic man who drove us to the ER seemed surprised I didn't want help getting my bruised and bloodied father inside, but he eventually shrugged and drove off after I tipped him more than was necessary. I declined to go into the emergency room with my father. I preferred to wait outside. Rose offered to accompany him. He put on a brave face and patted her shoulder, an inappropriately intimate gesture that fell somewhere between paternal and something else. He told her he would be fine on his own. She sighed as she watched him shuffle through the hissing pneumatic doors and into the lobby.

"Why didn't you tell me your father was an artist," she said, breathing into the word artist like he was some kind of secular saint.

"I told you, he checked out when I was little. And his paint-ings are popular for all the wrong reasons." An ambulance came screaming into the parking lot, and four EMS workers hauled a young black woman on a stretcher into the hospital, blood oozing from a deep gash in her forehead. The woman moaned loudly. Rose seemed not to notice.

"His work is popular?" she asked. "Who represents him? I think I might have seen a painting of his in Gallery Orange, actually? Does he have an agent?"

"Jesus, Rose. I don't know."

She sulked, pretending to read the news on her phone. Ac-tually I knew that Shuster & Cole had represented my father for the last nine years, and that his work was shown all over the Quarter, as well as at a place in Metairie, and at a gallery in Savannah. But these were not facts that Rose or anybody else would expect me to know. I was a scientist, after all, and a teacher. I had little use for art.

Science had allowed me to back away from the art world that was my father's domain; I always feigned disinterest about my father's rather prolific and successful painting ca-reer. As a doctoral student in ethnobotany I was not required to know anything about art. What I was required to know was that a special type of peptide, called a cyclotide, found in a rare species of algae could be used to augment antiretroviral therapies for HIV. I could be counted on to know that Inuit Native Americans living on Norton Sound in Alaska suffer almost none of the debilitating effects of antiretroviral drugs that ravage the general population, probably because a main component of their diet is salmon that eat the algae containing the cyclotides. I could also tell anyone interested that dental implants hurt like hell, because Dan, my former research assistant, took out my front tooth with a brick at the end of our expedition last year, right before I left him at a campground in the middle-of-nowhere Alaska, howling into the darkness. But Rose did not know about Dan or my ceramic tooth, and I could tell she only half listened when I talked about cyclotides and the Inuits and improving antiretroviral medications with algae.

We took a streetcar back to the apartment and got Rose's shiny new SUV to pick up the bikes from my father's lawn. The SUV was more practical, but we rode the bikes around town and to and from campus because they fit our image better. I hoisted the bikes into the trunk while Rose stared at my father's house as if it were a place of worship.

"How can his work be popular for the wrong reasons?" she asked. "If the paintings sell, that's the only reason that counts."

"That's not what you said before. You said real art is always misunderstood."

"I never said that."

In fact, she said it often, especially after the scathing faculty critiques of her food sculptures that left her in tears. But I could tell it did not matter. "Won't it be great, having your father live with us for a while? We'll be like one, big happy family," she continued dreamily.

"We can't be one big, happy family with only three people. Three's not a big family."

"So we'll just be one happy family, then," she said impatiently, gunning the engine. It was unfair. What she said made no sense, but she'd won the argument anyway.

THE FIRST TIME I met Rose she was selling pills at the back of an EDM concert in a warehouse near Magazine Street. I was only there to score something—I hated the throb of the music, and at thirty-three I was already feeling too old to be around the throng of stoned college kids dry humping each other on the dance floor. I spotted her standing at the back of the room, looking around with a kind of feigned disinterest that made me sure she was holding. She had a little of everything, and

I gave her fifty dollars for a little bag containing five Vicodin, three Oxycodone, and a Xany-bar.

A week later she answered my advertisement for a female roommate—students only—on Craigslist. I walked into the coffee shop on campus, looking for the self-described "fashionista with rad glasses." The way she sat at the table I could tell she was proud of her body and the way she looked, even from behind. She wore an electric blue, sleeveless silk blouse with a row of impossibly tiny, fabric-wrapped buttons marching up her back. And the glasses. Thick, red frames that pointed up slightly at the corners. I asked her where she bought her clothes, and she told me she made them. She moved in two days later. When the university cut my stipend and I couldn't cover my half of the rent, Rose called her parents in Southern California. They started writing the rent checks and mailing them directly to the property management company. That was six months ago. Rose still kept a sagging, tired futon in the room she had originally rented from me, but mostly she used it as a sewing room. When she came home with boys, she took them in there. When she came home with girls, she took them in there, too. But on most nights, we passed out together on the sofa, basking in the glow of whatever pharmaceuticals she brought home. When my father called earlier that morning, asking for help, I'd had to pry myself out of her beautifully thin and lightly muscled brown arms to take the call.

BY THE TIME WE got him back to the apartment, my father seemed much better. His face had been washed at the hospital, and it turned out that his nose was not broken after all. I did not ask him if he knew the men who had robbed him, but it was likely that he did. I remembered how when I was young, men often came to our small house in Metairie, looking for him. My mother would send me to bed, and I would watch from behind the curtains of my room as he left in a car with the men. He would reappear the next day, on the porch, or in the yard, or in the driveway, his body marked with the violence of the night before. It was something we had always shared, my father and I: an attraction to violence. Before Dan the research assistant with the brick, there had been Steve who almost broke my arm, and in high school there had been Walter who had split my lip over not wanting to take our date beyond third base. As I grew older I became convinced that my father had passed the victim trait on to me along with his predisposition to drink too much. People seemed to know they could hit us and get away with it.

As soon as my father stepped into the living room, he praised Rose's ridiculous fabric egg hanging over the sofa, admired her choice of materials, and noted the small size and the precision of the hand stitching around the edges of the thing. She was eating it up, gushing about how it was all about process, saying that with her important sculptures she did almost all the piecing by hand. I wanted to tell her to shut up. He nodded, knowingly, and asked her if she had any maquettes of her other sculptures. Maquettes! Couldn't he have just said models, like a normal person? I let Rose settle him in, and she proudly led him to her crappy room with the musty futon, where it had been agreed he would be staying. Rose and I would share my room while he was recovering, whatever that meant. He looked just fine to me. My face throbbed around the dental implant. Pain would be the dominant sensation in my face unless I did something to deal with it soon, and I had a stack of exams to grade that were already overdue. Last semester the department chair had made a point of telling me several students complained about my casual relationship with deadlines. I assumed this had something to do with my stipend being cut.

I had been grading the tests for over an hour when Rose came into the bedroom. My tooth still hurt like crazy, but I didn't care as much. I'd worked my way through the better part of a bottle of red wine. I was feeling a little more generous toward Rose and my father. So what if she liked his stupid paintings. So what if he noticed her tiny stitches. They both needed to feel like what they did was special. She was wearing pajamas made of matte crushed silk in a shade of brown so close to her skin tone that out of the corner of my eye she looked naked. I stared intently at my papers. I felt, as I often did in her presence, a little ashamed of my clothes. I was wearing a worn out old T-shirt that had once been a light hyacinth, but I had foolishly washed it with something red that turned it from delicate lavender to a fleshy, pinkish-blue, like the skin at the edge of a bruise. She had on the red eyeglasses, which meant she wanted to look smart. Rose had perfect vision. She climbed into bed next to me and held out her hand for my wine glass.

"You know," she said, "you're lucky." She took a long drink of my wine, then swished it around in the glass, and stared into it as if she could divine some meaning from the swirling red liquid. "Actually, more than lucky. Blessed. My father is on the other side of the country. I haven't seen him in months. But *your* father is here, staying with us. It's a gift."

Rose's family had immigrated to California from Shanxi

Province in China before she was born. Her father, a software engineer, encountered Mormon missionaries in the early seventies and ever since, the family had maintained ties to the Church of Latter-day Saints. He worked for a big tech company now, and he credited all his success to their faith. When she was feeling homesick, Rose saw blessings and gifts in everything. I'd never met Mr. and Mrs. Li, but I could easily picture their big house near the ocean, with its multi-level design and panoramic views. I often imagined the Lis saying prayers in their smart, modern living room, praying for the soul of their only daughter, who had gone away to New Orleans to make giant fast food out of cloth and do God only knew what else. Whenever Rose talked about blessings I always agreed with her, even when she was dead wrong.

"You're right," I said, and reclaimed my wine. She studied her short, neatly kept fingernails. She seemed to need more confirmation, so I added, "It's a blessing."

"I really like his paintings."

"Do you have any more Vicodin?" She shook her head, took off the cute glasses, and pulled the covers tightly around her body, swaddling herself and turning away from me. I wondered what her hair felt like, and for a moment I considered running my fingers through it. Instead I put down my papers, even though I hadn't finished with them yet, turned out the light and curled into a ball on the edge of my side of the mattress.

I woke up alone, my head aching a little from the wine. I looked around my room for evidence of Rose, but there was nothing. Even the covers on her side of the bed were smooth. As I biked to campus, I could not shake the feeling that I had somehow offended her. Why would she leave for the day without saying goodbye? Since we had become roommates she and I almost always rode in together, and it felt strange to make the trip alone.

MY FIRST CLASS of the day went badly. The students grumbled about not having their test scores—the last day to withdraw was approaching, and many of them feared that without a high mark on the exam, they would have no hope of passing. I snapped at one girl, telling her if she was that worried about her score she had probably failed already, and she should just drop now. I'd hoped to sound intimidating, but someone giggled in the back of the room, then another student said something to which the others around him laughed loudly. I sensed the classroom sliding out of my control and remembered a similar situation the previous semester that had ended with the students just leaving whenever they felt like it.

Teaching was a requirement of my fellowship, but it was not one of my strengths. I was at the university to research a family of plant-based cyclotides, uniquely shaped cells that have a three-dimensional spine, curved like a horseshoe. The open, middle part of the horseshoe is connected by nodes of circular protein, and their unique shape is extremely stable, making them good candidates for protecting cells from the degradation that can be caused by ongoing antiretroviral therapy. I was working with a species of cyclotide-rich algae unique to the waters of Norton Sound, Alaska. I'd become interested in the Sound after reading a paper on the treatment of an HIV outbreak in the Inuit population there. The Native Americans who lived on the Sound had responded exceptionally well to drugs such as Tenofovir and Ritonavir. There were no reported occurrences of liver failure and very low accounts of the nausea and extreme fatigue experienced by many patients. The circumstantial evidence suggested that their tolerance of the antiretroviral drugs could be due to a component of their diet: the local salmon that fed on the algae. I wanted to sample the algae in the Sound, culture it in the lab and develop a technique to extract the cyclotides in a usable, therapeutic form. The university was excited about this idea—plant-based pharmacology was hot. They assigned Dan, a graduate student studying botany, to the project as my research assistant and sent us to Alaska.

I had liked Alaska. I liked the sense of isolation, collecting tiny samples of the plants from the icy water by day, spending the freezing nights under a down comforter in Dan's sweaty arms. He'd insisted on holding me all night, and he would wake and complain if I got out of bed or moved. It had been my first project in the field, and even though things ended badly, I preferred that kind of work to dealing with students.

When the last students filed out of the lecture hall, I stood in the empty room and wondered if they disliked my class as much as I disliked teaching it. The room was thick with the youthful smell of their sweat, and I felt old. I pictured my hair graying as I stood behind that lectern, while class after class of uninterested pupils filled the seats in front of me. My face was beginning to glow with the familiar, persistent pain that the dental implant caused. I was starting to doubt that it would ever stop hurting. I decided to seek out Rose, who could always distract me from thinking too hard about where I might be in the next ten years.

Whenever I visited her in the sculpture department, Rose

tried to make me feel welcome, throwing her arms around me and introducing me as her roommate to all of her strangely dressed art student friends. But the chaos and scale of the place was unnerving. The building had an open floor plan, with different areas where students worked on their various projects. There were usually sparks flying and people shouting, but I could never tell what any of them were actually making. Today Rose was not in her sewing area. The beginnings of what might have been an oversized bucket of chicken constructed out of felt was taking form at her workbench. I followed the sound of her laugh around the corner.

She was perched on a packing crate with a skinny girl whose hair was spiky and dark. The girl had her arm around Rose's waist and they were laughing about something. Rose's eyes were squeezed shut and she was catching her breath in excited gasps. It was loud in the building, and neither of them noticed me. The girl whispered something to Rose I couldn't hear, and I noticed Rose's fingertips working quietly into the waist of the girl's black jeans. I recognized the girl and her pointy hair from my disastrous class last semester where the students had mutinied against me—she'd been one of the first to walk out. During my lectures she'd always had an impatient, bored look on her face, but with Rose she was shining. It filled me with a kind of despair, seeing them so happy, and I left without either of them realizing I'd come and gone.

When I came home, neither Rose's bike nor her SUV were out front and the door was not latched. My father was in the kitchen cooking some kind of stew in a pot. The air was heavy with Old Bay seasoning. He had turned off the air conditioning, and it was warmer than I liked in the house. On the table was a bottle of scotch, half full. He was chopping an onion and humming to himself. Aside from a few ugly bruises on his face, he looked good. Good enough, I thought, to go home. He pretended not to notice me as I crossed the room and pulled a beer out of the fridge.

"Where's Rose?" I asked. He raised his hands melodramatically, in something like a mea culpa gesture, scattering bits of onion all over the linoleum in the process.

"Ah. Amy. You missed her. I sent sweet Rose to go pick up some things for me."

"From your house?" I asked, not believing he would send my nineteen-year-old roommate into the Ninth Ward, to the house where he had just been robbed.

He started humming again and nodded his head in confirmation. He had a swagger to his movement, as if he were proud of having insinuated himself into my life and was now claiming the spaces of the house one by one: first Rose's sewing room, now the kitchen.

"Hey," I said, and grabbed his arm to make him stop chopping the onions. His whole body tensed.

"There's nothing good going to come from you putting your hands on me, Amelia."

I took my hand off him instinctively, as if hearing my full name forced me to obey him. "I raised you better than that," he went on.

Of course, he hadn't. He'd been admitted to State when I was fourteen, and his presence in my life had been intermittent after that, at best. Still, he held some strange sway over me, and I resigned myself to sitting at the kitchen table and peeling the label off my beer.

"How long are you staying?" I asked, without looking at him. He tossed the onions into my large skillet; they crackled in the hot oil.

"That's not any way to treat family. But if you want me to go, I'll leave any time. I'll just tell your little girlfriend you'd rather put me out than put up with me, and that will be that. I'll go."

I got up to leave, to go somewhere in the apartment where he was not.

By eleven, Rose was still not home. Had something happened when she went to get my father's things? Was she out with the spiky hair girl, or back at the sculpture studio? My father had retreated to what was now his room. I had refused to have any of his stew, even though it smelled delicious. I didn't want him thinking I was being friendly. Close to midnight I heard Rose pull up in front of the house. She had never really learned to parallel park and always drove over the curb a little. I picked up the small stack of exams I had saved to grade when she got back, so she wouldn't know I'd been waiting for her to come home all night. She came in carrying a large bundle of rolled up canvas and a toolbox splattered with paint, no doubt rescued from my father's house. She immediately responded to the smell of the stew, sniffing the air and making deeply appreciative groans of pleasure I thought were excessive.

"Oh Amy. Something smells amazing. Does your dad cook, too?"

"I looked for you at the studio today."

"I left early."

She carefully put my father's painting supplies down on the floor, smoothing the canvas, making sure the latches on the box were secure.

"I was there early."

I could hear the embarrassingly peevish tone in my voice, but Rose seemed not to notice. She was already floating away from me toward the kitchen. She returned with a large glass of ice water. When she sat down next to me, she leaned in close and spoke in a whisper. Her pupils were large and black, and her skin shimmered with sweat.

"Hey. I got something from a girl at school. It's fabulous. Like that Ecstasy we had last month, but not so speedy."

"I can't. I mean I'd like to. I need to go in early tomorrow."

Rose shrugged and headed into my bedroom. I'd expected her to try a little harder to change my mind. I spent the rest of the night on the sofa, but slept fitfully, hoping she would reappear and ask me to come back into my room. By three in the morning I had decided that if she offered again, I would take whatever she had. At one point I woke up, sensing someone in the room, but it was only my father, collecting his paints.

I posted the exam scores the next morning, early enough for the students to see them before class. When I looked over the classroom, I noticed many empty seats. I estimated about a quarter of them had dropped. Good. Less papers for me to grade. I wondered what Rose acted like in her classes that were not art-related. I was sure that if she had been one of my students, we would not be friends and we would definitely not live together. I was giving my standard lecture on mitosis, but my mind was wandering. I was thinking that Rose and I should get away for a while, maybe take a vacation somewhere over the upcoming summer break, when I got a glimpse of a boy's laptop. I thought he had been taking notes, but actually he was texting. I announced I was banning all laptops for the rest of the semester. Their faces fell, and a murmur of disbelief swept through the room. But what did it matter if they despised me. We only had to tolerate another two months together, and then everyone could go their separate ways.

When I got back to the house that night, the front door was not only unlocked, but ajar. I heard their voices before I saw them. Rose was talking about her food sculptures. I could tell because of her energized yet wistful way of speaking. Each sentence lifted up at the end, like a question that wasn't really a question. I removed my shoes in the living room and walked down the hall in my socks.

"So, the size, the scale, I mean? It's all about our appetites, how they've grown out of control. How we've become outpaced by our desires." There was some murmured response. "And, you know, it's the things that aren't good for us that we want the most?" She sounded like she was really on quite a tear, like she had taken something—I had no idea what. I walked into the room and saw her, topless, seated on a chair, while my father sketched her on a huge canvas. I had never seen Rose topless before. She turned to face me when I entered the room, and I saw that between her perfect breasts was a long, red scar that ran the length of her sternum. She smiled.

I told her she was imposing on me by insisting that my father stay with us. I told her that her sense of ridiculous filial piety—no doubt stemming from some Confucian philosophy embedded in her genetic code—had mixed with her inane idea of his presence being a blessing, and now he was getting her to take her clothes off, flattering her by telling her she could be a real artist, instead of a spoiled brat playing with a sewing machine. It was a bad choice of words, and I regretted the last sentence even before I finished saying it. She called me a racist and cried as she ran out into the night, got into her car and left.

Rose did not come home that night. I woke up late, still on the sofa where I had been waiting for her, ready to say I was sorry, that I needed her, that she was the most brilliant person I had ever met and that I wanted to make things okay between us. I went through the first class of the day on autopilot. I was too busy thinking about Rose to find time to hate my students, or to worry about the email from the department chair in my inbox that I had been afraid to open, with the subject line, "Research Requirements of your Fellowship."

I drove home at lunchtime, hoping she was there. The house was locked. Once inside, I saw that her fabric egg was no longer over the sofa. I opened the door to her sewing room—it was empty, except for the futon, and my father's things, his paints and the half-started sketch of her. All her strange and beautiful clothes were gone from the closet.

My father was in the kitchen. He was hunched over the sink, washing the dishes. He had never cleaned anything when I was a girl, unless he was trying to make up with my mother. He nodded his head in acknowledgement as I walked in. I sat at the table, staring at my hands. My nails needed cleaning.

"She asked me to draw her, you know. She said I'd like her scar," he said. I nodded. "It wasn't my idea, Amy."

"I'm sure."

"I can stay until you find another roommate. That way you won't be alone," he said. I must have groaned, because he turned to me, took my hand and smiled, trying to cheer me up. "Look. Everything will be fine. You and me, we're a family, remember?"

II.

PRAIRIE

A Screenplay

FADE IN:

EXT. PRAIRIE - MORNING

Expansive WHEAT FIELDS sway under an endless blue sky.

A worn two-lane HIGHWAY cuts through the fields. The only sound is the WIND.

CARD OVER: OUTSIDE OF BOZEMAN, MONTANA.

Red-tailed HAWKS skim over the tops of the wheat.

The sound of an ENGINE in the distance.

ON A HAWK

Perched on an old fence post. The ENGINE sound grows louder.

The hawk SHRIEKS and flies away.

An expensive BLACK CAR ROARS past the fence post and is gone.

TITLE CARD: PRAIRIE

INT. CABIN - MORNING

Faded floral wallpaper. A wood-burning stove in the corner. The only illumination is SUNLIGHT filtered through dirty windowpanes. Cardboard boxes, half packed, are everywhere.

SAL, ninety, a weathered old post of a man, sits alone at a
table covered in old photographs and papers. He stares at a
TICKING CLOCK over the mantel.

INT. CAR - MORNING

The interior of the car is immaculate and dark. The golden
prairie slides past the window behind a MAN wearing
black sunglasses.

CALEB, forty, has dark hair, tailored clothes and looks like
he's accustomed to getting what he wants. He checks the
time on a heavy, expensive watch.

Caleb bears down on the gas; the engine ROARS.

EXT. CABIN - DAY

The ramshackle CABIN is surrounded by an ocean of rolling
PRAIRIE. An old black BARN, in even greater disrepair,
leans to one side behind it.

The ENGINE can be heard faintly in the distance.

INT. CABIN - DAY

Sal sucks on a CHAW of tobacco. He SPITS into an old can on
the floor.

EXT. CABIN - DAY

Kicking up a huge cloud of dust, Caleb's car grinds to a halt
in front of the cabin.

INT. CABIN - DAY

Sal listens as the engine is cut. He picks up a double-barrel
    Smith & Wesson from beside his chair.

CLACK! Sal cocks the weapon and points it at the DOOR, just
    as it is opened by Caleb.

> SAL
> (fiercely)
> You can't have it. You think you've
> won, but the game's not over yet.

Caleb takes off his sunglasses and looks around the room
    with an appraising gaze.

> CALEB
> You're not packed.

Sal keeps the gun trained on Caleb. Caleb doesn't notice or
    doesn't care. He picks up a rusty RABBIT TRAP and places
    it into an almost full box.

> CALEB (CONT'D)
> Dad. I know you remember.

Sal looks confused. He doesn't know who Caleb is. Caleb lays
    his hand on Sal's shoulder.

> CALEB (CONT'D)
> Dad.

(A beat. Then louder.)

Sal.

A flash of recognition in Sal's rheumy eyes. He lowers the
gun.

SAL
Caleb. I'm sorry. Slipped my mind.

Caleb sighs and begins closing up boxes.

CALEB
Just help me.

Sal doesn't move. Caleb places items into a box: first the clock
from the mantel, then a few tattered books. Everything is
so dusty that when an item is removed its outline remains
behind.

SAL
Caleb, I can't go. We can't trust 'em.
They're liable to steal everything.

CALEB
The movers won't steal your things.
Promise.

Caleb continues packing up the contents of the room. He
takes the teakettle off the stove, empties the contents into
the sink with a loud SPLASH.

SAL

You're in on it too, now, I reckon.

Sal begins to sob silently. His body trembles, his veneer of
toughness cracks. He's undone.

Caleb lays a comforting hand on Sal's shoulder. The old man
brushes him away.

SAL (CONT'D)

Just get the hell out of my house!

Caleb tries a new approach. He starts going through a pile of
photographs on the table.

CALEB

I never knew you had all these old
photos. We should put some in
frames, you know? Hang them up
at the new place.

Sal is breathing heavy and leaning back in his chair. He
ignores Caleb.

Caleb shuffles through the pile and produces a photo.

IN THE PHOTOGRAPH:

Two teenage boys, one tall with fair hair and one shorter and
    thicker with dark hair, standing by a massive tractor. The
    taller boy wears an easy, charismatic smile. The shorter boy
    looks angry.

> CALEB (CONT'D)
> Hey, this must be your brother.
> Silas, right?

Rocking back and forth in the chair, Sal grits his teeth and
    squeezes back tears.

> SAL
> I told you to get out!

Sal's rocking overturns the tobacco spit can. It slops nasty
    brown liquid onto Caleb's polished black shoe.

Caleb ignores the mess. He finds another photograph and
    waves it in front of Sal, hoping to get his attention.

IN THE PHOTOGRAPH:

The darker, smaller boy from the other picture is standing
    in front of the barn with a RED-TAILED PRAIRIE HAWK
    perched on his gloved hand. The boy is smiling.

CALEB

Dad, look at this one. You never
told me you had a bird.

Sal stops rocking and un-squints his eyes. He looks at the
picture, his face softens.

SAL
(whispers)

Prairie.

CALEB
(infinitely patient, like talking to a child)
No, dad. The bird.

Sal gives Caleb a condescending look. He's completely lucid
now.

SAL

Prairie was the bird's name. Her
name.

CALEB

Tell me about her. Tell me about
Prairie.

Again, Sal closes his eyes. Caleb waits. Caleb quietly begins
placing the other photos into a box. Sal senses what he's up
to without opening his eyes.

                            SAL

          Caleb, if you want to hear about
          Prairie Bird, you better stop packin'
          up all my things on the sly.

Caleb stops packing the photos, sits down in front of his
    father with a sigh.

                           CALEB

              All right.

Sal opens his eyes and leans forward, taking a long look at the
    faded photograph.

DISSOLVE TO:

EXT. MONTANA PRAIRIE - DAY - THE PAST

Everything looks just like the landscape we saw earlier, the
    WIND even sounds the same as it stirs the tall grasses.
    Suddenly the BANG of a shotgun tears through the
    landscape. WINGS beat the air as a clutch of pheasants
    scatter up and out of the grass.

                         SAL (V.O.)

          I was out with Silas, hunting
          pheasant.

SILAS, 17, the taller, fair boy from the photograph, rises up
    from the grasses holding a smoking GUN.

SAL, 14, the smaller, darker boy, stands behind his brother, looking uneasy.

A HAWK circles around the boys and SHRIEKS. It's a piercing cry. Sal covers his ears. The hawk continues to circle, shrieking.

Silas cocks the weapon, aims for the hawk and pulls the trigger. BANG! The hawk falls from the sky, dead. Sal GASPS. Silas turns around shoots him a predatory smile.

> SAL (V.O.)
> A hawk came by, and Silas shot her.
> By accident, of course.

The boys walk over to where the hawk fell, and Silas KICKS its limp body, first lightly then hard. Every time Silas kicks the bird Sal flinches.

A PEEPING sound cuts over the grass. Silas stops his assault on the dead bird and walks toward the sound.

The PEEPING sound continues, emanating from a whorl of prairie grass. Silas parts the grass and we see:

A BABY HAWK

Small and downy, more like a cotton ball with black eyes and a yellow mouth than anything else.

SAL (V.O.)
The hawk's chick was nearby. I
suppose she was tryn' to give us a
scare, so's we'd leave them both be.

LOOKING UP FROM THE CHICK'S POV:

Framed by the tall grass, Silas raises his boot, about to stomp
   down, a smile twisting the corner of his mouth.

The baby hawk PEEPS loudly.

Sal punches Silas square in the jaw, sending him flying. Sal
   scoops up the little bird.

SAL (V.O.)
Silas didn't reckon it was a good
idea, takin' wild animals home. But
I didn't care.

Sal cradles the little bird close to his chest. The little creature
   nestles into him.

A WIDER ANGLE

Shows Sal holding the bird as Silas stalks off through the
   grass. The countryside is expansive. They are the only
   living souls for miles.

The sound of a RINGING CELL PHONE is heard.

CUT TO:

INT. CABIN - DAY - PRESENT DAY

Caleb pulls the ringing cell phone from his pocket.

> CALEB
>
> Just a sec.
>> (into phone)
>
> Yes? Yes, I'm at the property now.

Sal is watching his son with a sharp gaze. Telling his story has forced him to gather his wits. Caleb absently begins putting more things into boxes as he talks.

> CALEB (CONT'D)
>> (into phone)
>
> Actually, you think you can hold
> back about, oh, another hour? Even
> two? Yeah. All right.

Caleb hangs up and looks down at his father.

Sal stares back at him.

> CALEB (CONT'D)
>
> I know this isn't what you wanted.
> But it's got to happen.

Sal defiantly crosses his arms and turns toward the wall.

Caleb hunkers down in front of him.

> CALEB (CONT'D)
>
> Finish telling me about Prairie
> while I pack? All you have to do is
> talk, and sit.

Sal knows the move is inevitable. He nods his head in agreement.

Caleb smiles at his father.

> CALEB (CONT'D)
>
> Thanks.

Caleb gets back to packing and turns on what looks to be the only electric light in the room, a bare lightbulb hanging from the ceiling.

THE LIGHTBULB

Glows yellow.

DISSOLVE TO:

INT. CABIN - NIGHT - THE PAST

An old-fashioned, filament lightbulb GLOWS in the cabin. The wallpaper is bright and everything is in order.

AGATHA, Sal's mother, a young woman with fair hair pulled back into a tightly wound bun, has just turned on the light and now places a pan of steaming ROLLS on the table.

> SAL (V.O.)
> Silas may not have cared for it
> too much, but Mama loved havin'
> Prairie Bird around.

Sal sits near the fireplace with Prairie, now a fledgling with
    feathers as well as down. She perches on a small log.
    Agatha smiles warmly at Sal. Sal smiles back. He loves her.

Sal WHISTLES as he holds a small piece of dried meat out for
    Prairie, who takes it from his fingers.

> SAL (V.O.)
> She was always real nice to us boys
> after Pa left. Always tried to let us
> have our way.

ON SAL'S HAND

He strokes Prairie's head. She bites. Sal's finger BLEEDS. Sal
    winces but doesn't pull away.

Prairie lets go.

The cabin door OPENS with force, and Silas enters. Behind
    him, snow sweeps in. Silas closes door, hard.

SAL looks gently at Agatha. She looks away. She's afraid of
    Silas.

>   CALEB (V.O.)
>   So, how'd you tame her?

Silas strides over to the pan of rolls and takes one. He takes a
   bite, chews, then spits it out. Agatha recoils. Sal starts to get
   up but Agatha signals for him to stop.

>   SAL (V.O.)
>   Patience. Love. And dried venison,
>   naturally.

The wind whistles.

ON PRAIRIE:

Her eyes glint in the firelight.

INT. CABIN BEDROOM - NIGHT

Sal and Silas in twin beds across the room from each other.
   The room is bare and plain, the walls made of rough board.
   The beds are covered with handmade quilts. A single
   candle burns on the nightstand between them. Prairie sits,
   tethered by a thin leather strap to a perch standing at the
   foot of Sal's bed.

>   SAL (V.O.)
>   I kept Prairie inside all winter long.
>   Guess she figured she was stuck
>   with me.

Silas motions for Sal to come over to his bed. Sal shakes his
head NO.

                    SAL (V.O.)
          Of course Silas and me shared a
          room, so really we were all stuck
          with each other.

Silas holds his finger to his lips for SILENCE and motions Sal
over again.

Sal comes over and kneels on Silas' bed reluctantly. Bed
springs SQUEAK. Silas holds his finger over his lips again,
then pulls a CORK out of a knothole in the wall.

THROUGH THE HOLE

Agatha taking off her dress. Her pale breasts shine in the
candlelight. Unwound, her long yellow hair flows down
her back.

Sal gasps and snatches the cork from Silas, shoving it back in.

Silas laughs.

Prairie flaps wildly around her perch, tries to fly, but is
snapped back by the tether.

Sal extinguishes the candle and quickly gets back into his
own bed. Silas keeps laughing softly but insidiously. Sal
covers his ears in the darkness.

EXT. MONTANA PRAIRIE - DAY

The same idyllic, expansive setting we've been looking at all
    along.

> SAL (V.O.)
> Come spring, I took her out and
> taught her to hunt.

A DEAD BABY RABBIT CAUGHT IN A TRAP

Sal carefully opens the trap. Prairie is on his shoulder and is
    very interested. She's an adult now and has lost all of her
    baby fluff.

> CALEB (V.O.)
> That must've been something.

Sal puts Prairie on the ground. He ties a length of string to the
    rabbit's leg and swings it over his head in an arc, making
    the same WHISTLING sound he made while feeding
    Prairie in the cabin.

> SAL (V.O.)
> She was a vision.

Prairie SHRIEKS and gets herself airborne. She swoops after
    the rabbit and catches it midair in her sharp, curved talons.

I/E. BARN LOFT - DAY

A high barn loft that is open to the prairie. The expected worn timbers and straw on the planks. One corner of the loft has been partitioned off with chicken wire to make a cage for Prairie.

Outside of the cage a wooden post has been set up for Prairie, and she waits there expectantly.

Sal WHISTLES as he swings a rabbit on a string, building up momentum before sending it out the front of the barn.

Prairie is after it in a flash.

ON PRAIRIE

The bird catches the rabbit and SWOOPS onto a tree branch. She tears at its flesh and eats.

PRAIRIE'S TALONS AND BEAK are covered in the rabbit's BLOOD.

IN THE LOFT

Silas climbs up the ladder into the loft behind Sal. Sal is still looking after the bird and doesn't hear him come up. Silas SHOVES Sal, and he stumbles, almost falling out of the barn loft.

SAL'S POV:

Looking down over the edge of the barn we see a wheat
thresher very far down. The curved blades on the machine
look menacing, lethal.

Silas smiles his twisted smile.

Sal charges him head on. Silas goes down and the boys
wrestle fiercely. Silas is quick and cunning, and he soon has
Sal by the throat.

ON SAL

Choking and struggling to catch his breath.

ON SILAS

Laughing at his brother's pain.

Suddenly with a SHRIEK Prairie flies in, slashing a long cut
down Silas's cheek with her talons.

Silas cries out and holds his face. He takes his hand away and
looks at it in disbelief.

ON SILAS'S HAND

Bright red BLOOD.

Silas looks around for Prairie, but she's gone. Still on the
floor, Sal coughs.

SILAS

Bastard! You know what you are?
It's true. It's why he left.

Sal just coughs. Silas SPITS on him.

The WHISTLING sound of a teakettle cuts through the air.

CUT TO:

INT. CABIN - AFTERNOON - PRESENT DAY

The WHISTLING sound is even louder.

SAL'S WRINKLED EYES snap open. He looks around wildly.

THE BATTERED TEAKETTLE is taken off the stove by Caleb.

His shirt sleeves are rolled up, and he's grimy and sweaty
    from packing. He pours steaming water over a tea bag for
    Sal.

CALEB

Figured I'd just let you sleep.

A WIDER ANGLE

Reveals that the entire cabin has been packed, save a couple
    of kerosene lamps that, with the bare lightbulb, provide the
    only illumination.

Sal is disoriented; he reaches for his gun; it's not there.

CALEB (CONT'D)
Packed that, too.

Sal looks for a moment like he might break down again, but he pulls it together.

Caleb pours himself some tea and sits down.

CALEB (CONT'D)
So what finally happened to her?
Prairie?

EXT. MONTANA PRAIRIE - EVENING - THE PAST

The fields are as golden as ever. The setting sun brings out the orange and gold of the wheat.

Sal drives a huge TRACTOR pulling the thresher down the gravel road towards the cabin.

SAL (V.O.)
After Pa left, we struggled. Us
boys couldn't really work the farm
proper on our own, couldn't get
enough wheat harvested to keep
the bills paid. I left to hire out
our thresher to a farmer on the
other side of Bozeman, just to earn
enough to make the payments on
the land.

Sal pulls up beside the cabin.

> SAL (V.O.)
> I was gone about a week. Mama
> said not to worry about leaving.
> Said everything would be fine.

Sal walks into the cabin. It's a mess. Dishes in the sink, on the table. Agatha is at the table, reading silently from a worn black BIBLE.

She looks up, her face battered and BRUISED.

> SAL (V.O.)
> I should have known better.

Sal doesn't say a word. He RUNS out of the cabin toward the barn.

I/E. BARN LOFT - EVENING

Sal climbs the ladder into the loft at triple speed. He steps into the loft and finds Silas there, as if waiting for him. There is no sign of Prairie.

> CALEB (V.O.)
> What happened?

Sal stares at his brother. He can barely contain his rage.

SAL (V.O.)

I'm really not sure. He drove her
off, somehow. By the time I got
back, Prairie was long gone.

Standing silhouetted against the darkening sky, Silas
LAUGHS.

SILAS

She's gone, little bastard.

Silas turns his back on Sal and gestures out the open hangar
doors.

SILAS (CONT'D)

She's out there, somewhere.

Sal CHARGES at Silas and knocks him OUT of the hangar
doors. The only sound Silas makes is a GRUNT of surprise
when hit.

With a meaty THUD, Silas hits the ground below.

Sal stands silhouetted in front of the night dark sky looking
out. He WHISTLES for Prairie.

SAL (V.O.)

I always had a feelin' she was
near, but I could never be sure. He
turned her from people, I reckon.

> CALEB (V.O.)
> Silas wouldn't tell you what
> happened?

EXT. BARN - EVENING

Silas's lifeless body lies on the hard packed dirt in front of the
barn. BLOOD from his nose and mouth pool in the dust.
Sal can still be heard WHISTLING for Prairie off camera.

> SAL (V.O.)
> Never got the chance. Not long
> after she disappeared, Silas fell
> from the old barn.

> CALEB (V.O.)
> Jesus, Dad.

INT. CABIN - MOMENTS LATER

Agatha looks up from her BIBLE and sees Sal in the door,
tears running down his face. She goes to him and they hold
each other.

The loud sound of a CAR HORN penetrates the silence.

CUT TO:

INT. CABIN - LATE AFTERNOON - PRESENT DAY

The horn BLARES in the cabin. Sal and Caleb look at each
other. They both look worn out.

CALEB

That'll be the movers.

They both get up, Sal with some difficulty. All the boxes are
neatly stacked. Sal leaves the photo of him and Prairie on
the table. Caleb picks it up.

CALEB (CONT'D)

Dad, don't you want your photo?

SAL

Leave it.

Caleb shrugs and puts the photo back down on the table. He
pulls the string on the lightbulb, shutting it off. The cabin is
dark.

EXT. CABIN - LATE AFTERNOON

A BIRD'S-EYE VIEW

Shows the cabin, with Sal hobbling out of it. There's a big
moving van pulled up in the drive next to Caleb's black car.

From our high vantage point the old barn looms, its long
shadow creeping toward the house.

The wheat is gold and orange in the evening sun. As we drift
ever upwards, a hawk's SHRIEK is heard.

PRAIRIE

Caleb's black car, tiny now, drives away on the gravel road
until it's completely out of sight.

FADE OUT.

III.

THE MOMMIES

WE ARE THE MOMMIES. We're all still young, or young enough, and we are very, very hip. We only have one child, so far. Our group meets every Wednesday, for baby-centered fun, snacks and play. We're expert mothers. If you find yourself in need of parenting advice, you can refer to our online posts. Our screen names are Mommylicious, SweetBabyLove, Mamaholic, and HotMilk28. You can read our comments on BabyZone.com and TheMommyNest.net under topics such as *Is baby eating enough?* (probably not) and *Weaning from the breast—is my toddler ready?* (What kind of mother would rush her toddler to stop nursing?) And, *Getting rid of stretch marks.* (If you're concerned about superficial things like stretch marks, you shouldn't be posting on a holistic parenting site.)

Our real names are Kendra, Adrian, Mica, and Ashley. We met at an attachment parenting class at a breastfeeding support boutique. Now we meet every week at one of our homes, which is great because we can have the entire afternoon to spend with each other and our darling children. Sometimes one of us will invite another mother to one of our meetings — but they are never as dedicated to natural parenting as we are; many of them aren't even stay-at-home moms. We're all relieved when they leave and don't come back. Of course we never say this out loud — we're too nice.

WE'VE BEEN PLANNING to be perfect mommies for a long time. We all made sure to give our babies the right kind of names. Studies have shown this really matters — what you call a child will affect not only their likability, but their lifelong success. Did you know that almost seventy-five percent of boys named Kevin are convicted of a felony before they turn thirty? The ideal name should be uncommon enough to sound original, but not too weird or overly ethnic. Something in the top hundred but not the top twenty is best. Adrian named her son Oscar, which according to the census bureau is currently the thirtieth most popular name for boys. Names with a literary connection have the added bonus of showing off how well-read the parents are; Mica's little girl is named Harper. Old-lady names for girls are also trending, and for good reason. What better way to announce to the world that you have a timeless sense of style and are not subject to current fads than to name your daughter Eunice, as Ashley did. Kendra's son is named Noah—the Old Testament is hot right now, for obvious reasons.

To an outsider, it might seem we're overly focused on our roles as mothers, that we have no interests besides being exceptional, perfect parents. Not so! We have degrees in anthropology, sociology, English literature, and studio art. It is true that we quit our jobs as bank tellers, restaurant general managers, data-entry specialists, and ESL tutors so we can stay home, but this was our choice. After all, even the most liberated women understand that young children benefit from having one parent at home full time. Yes, it's a sacrifice, but when you see how healthy and well-adjusted your free-range, organic baby looks next to the runny-nosed, pre-schooled children of working mothers, you realize it's all worth it and you've made the right decision. Besides, our husbands work. Our husbands are hip, too; Adrian and Mica's husbands have beards. They love us unconditionally. We love them, too, but our babies come first, and our husbands understand that. What our husbands do for work is not important; they have jobs we find boring. They are not invited to our meetings.

WE'VE BEEN MEETING for about six months, and most of the babies eat solid food now, in addition to nursing. We are committed to feeding them only organic, non-GMO, conflict-free fruits and vegetables. Eating nonorganic vegetables can lead to autism. Mica is the most dedicated—Harper's food is always made from produce that is not only fresh, but local. Because of this she is the de-facto group leader. You've probably seen her shopping at the farmers' market lately, eleven-month-old Harper, howling and kicking, swaddled on her hip. Mica is never embarrassed; public tantrums are a sign that baby is developing a sense of individuality. She just gives Harper gentle kisses on her forehead and lets her yank out handfuls of her hair while she focuses on picking out the best sugar beets, carrots and turnips—it's winter so root vegetables are about the only thing available locally. Mica allots three hours each day to steam and process fresh food for Harper. As we all know, fresh is best, so performing the task daily is worth the extra effort.

Adrian, on the other hand, is very lazy when it comes to baby food. She buys the little squeezable, single-serve portions of organic baby purees. But then, we expected her to. She stopped letting little Oscar nurse just because he got his first tooth—she only pumps now. Our lactation consultants have warned us that pumping exclusively can cause low milk production, which can lead to supplementing with formula. And it's a well-known fact that exclusively breastfed babies are superior to babies fed with formula in every possible way—they are smarter, healthier, and prettier.

Our babies use cloth diapers. The only time we ever use disposables is for travel, and even then we use the organic, biodegradable kind. Unfortunately, the diapers are so environmentally friendly that they often begin to biodegrade while still on the baby, so this means mommy has to do a diaper change about every hour. Cloth diapering is easy, as long as you don't mind dedicating a portion of each day to spraying them off with a hose you hook up to your washing machine. It's not fun, we will admit, but it's worth it in the long run. Do you know the difference between cloth-diapered babies and the ones that use disposables? Obviously, their butts are smarter.

●

THE MOMMIES

TODAY WE ARE HAVING a birthday party for Mica's baby, Harper, who is turning one. We are serving homemade lemonade and beer from the local microbrewery and whiskey sours served in mason jars. We bought a case of Chardonnay from a local winery, even though it tastes awful. We have made cupcakes — both the regular kind and gluten free. Adrian can't tolerate gluten. All of our childless friends have been invited so they can marvel at how much we've got it together and worship at the altar of our maternal bliss. Everyone in our group loves parties because they give us an excuse to drink too much wine and talk about the wonderful journey of motherhood, starting with the birth experience. We all gave birth naturally, sans anesthesia. Except for Kendra. She got an epidural, but only after forty-three hours of natural labor. Each of us thinks, privately, that we would have held out longer. We've read about the bad effects of anesthesia on baby's brain and suspect that Kendra's epidural is probably the reason her child has yet to say more than three words. We love telling people that our babies were delivered vaginally. We know the V-word makes many people uncomfortable, and we relish having that power over them. Drinks in hand, we corner Mica's mother and father.

"You must be so proud that Harper was delivered *vaginally*," we say.

They smile and nod politely, but we can tell they want the afternoon to be over. We stare down our single friends while we tell our birth stories, daring them to change the subject. They never do.

Our husbands drink the whisky sours from the mason jars and show each other hot photos of us in our nursing lingerie on their iPhones. They joke with each other about how they never get laid anymore, and they chase the kids across Kendra's fair-trade organic wool rug, grabbing them by the legs and making them squeal with delight. After a while we remind them in our best mommy voices, "We are *gentle* with baby." They sulk but relent and go into the kitchen to pour more drinks.

Mica opens Harper's presents—Harper is asleep in the guest bedroom after a long crying jag. The childless guests mostly bring toys. The presents are for Mica and Harper, but we all sit near her and *ooh* and *ahh* over the gifts as if they are for us. Mica's parents have brought an especially thoughtful gift; a set of finger paints made from organic, nontoxic vegetable dye. They've obviously made an effort—good for them. But the crown jewel of all the presents is our gift to Mica: the BioButt© starter kit. You use it to compost the contents of baby's dirty diapers into organic fertilizer for your garden. We all pour another drink to congratulate ourselves because we know we've chosen the perfect gift—useful, sustainable, and gender-neutral. Mica loves it. The only bad gift is from Mica's friend, Tony, a book titled *Disciplining Your Toddler Without Shouting or Spanking*. Poor Tony. He obviously doesn't know that Mica practices Empowerment Parenting, which means Harper will never hear the word *no* until she is at least ten years old.

On the drive home, we are flush with wine and motherly pride.

"Wasn't that party the best?" we say to our husbands, as we ride home in our Subaru Foresters, NPR whispering softly on the radio so as not to wake our sleeping babies. They only grunt in response, but we forgive them for being less enthusiastic than we are. We are realizing that being mothers is our purpose, our calling—something we share with each other, and not with our men.

That night we nurse our babies while our husbands snore beside us in bed, their bourbon-scented breath making the air hot and musky. We worry that as our little ones grow, they will need us less. All too soon, they will stop nursing. Eventually they will go off to school, and then we will be forced to do something else, to get our master's degrees, or go back to our jobs that we hated. There is only one solution to this problem, we decide. Soon, it will be time to have another baby.

BAD SIGNS

WATCHING THE ANGULAR SHAPE of his shoulders shift under the weight of his pack, I followed Jacob along the trail. The tops of his pale arms were a raw, violated pink from yesterday's sunburn, and his breathing was labored as he made his way up the rocky path. Even from behind, my stepson looked like he needed my protection. Jacob was seventeen and asthmatic, and we had been on the mountain for five days. I knew if he turned around I would not be able to avoid staring at the un-natural cavity in his chest: a cup-shaped depression where his breastbone dipped suddenly in. The sunken part of him was about the width and depth of an apple. Before I met Jacob, his father warned me about his strange appearance. A harmless, congenital defect of the sternum is how Stephen described his son's deformity. It frightened me at first, and even after knowing Jacob for seven years, looking at it made me uneasy.

JACOB THOUGHT HIS FATHER'S disappearance was my fault, but he didn't know anything. How can any one person ever be responsible for another? I wanted to explain this to him, but every time I went over what I might say to him in my head, it sounded like a list of excuses. So instead I fell back on the now-familiar phrases the cognitive therapist told me to say when the accusations that I drove Stephen off came fast and furious from this boy who was not my son. *I loved your father. I don't know why he left.* If all else failed, I'd try telling the boy that Stephen could still come back. I knew this was unlikely, but it would shut him up for a little while, at least. It bought me time.

Before we went up the mountain, these conversations would often begin in the kitchen and finish at the edge of the forest behind our house, with me calling up into the branches of one of the dark pines he'd climbed to hide himself. Since his father disappeared, Jacob had developed a habit of starting an argument with me and then running away into the trees, forcing me to find him. I had been advised to try to break this pattern—both my therapist and Jacob's current counselor had cautioned me about rewarding my stepson's undesirable behavior by chasing him. But I always followed anyway.

IN THE SPORTING GOODS STORE where we purchased our supplies for the hiking trip, people looked at us strangely. No doubt this was because I was almost fifty and Jacob, who was still a boy but not a child, insisted on being too close to me in the store. He wanted to hold my hand so I let him, his slim fingers cool against my palm. When he spotted something he liked, a small but expensive camp stove or a hi-loft down sleeping bag, he would put his arm around my waist and draw me toward the item in an overly intimate manner, as if I were his lover instead of his father's former wife. When we finally assembled our haul of gear at the counter, the salesclerk, a bearded man in his sixties with thick fingers, jerked his head in Jacob's direction and asked me skeptically, "He's your son?"

Wishing for the thousandth time that Jacob's real mother was available to take him off my hands, I gave the clerk what Stephen had referred to as *the look* and slapped down my credit card.

•

THE FIRST SUMMER I lived with Jacob, he had just turned ten and refused to wear shoes. Stephen and I were moving into the house we bought after knowing each other for six months. A big A-frame with exposed beams and a massive kitchen with lots of windows, it looked like a house where anything would be possible—even a marriage to a man I had known less than a year with a son who I feared would never truly be mine. The morning we pulled up to the house in the rented moving truck, Jacob jumped from the cab before the engine was off and ran to the back edge of the property. I ran after, just in time to see him climbing the largest pine behind the house, a hunting knife gripped between his teeth. Stephen said nothing, did nothing—like this was normal—so I followed his lead. Jacob carved shallow notches in the branches of the tree, and then set up little buckets under the cuts. The next day he collected the sap and rubbed the soles of his feet with it. I was alone in the kitchen when he came in, tracking sticky, pine-smelling footprints on the floor. He announced that he was conditioning his feet to be tough, like an animal's. Shirtless, the hollow in his chest rising and falling with the rhythm of his breath, he already looked feral. It seemed like a bad idea to upset him—

Stephen had warned me that Jacob was prone to crippling asthma attacks when he became agitated.

"If you want your feet to become strong, like an animal's, just pine sap won't be enough."

"What do you know about it?" he said.

"You need to wash them in the cold water from the stream that comes down the mountain." His eyes were locked on me, so I kept going. "And you should mix the sap with the red clay from the creek bank before you put it on."

"Bullshit," he said, smiling. I was sure I'd blown it, that he'd seen through my clumsy attempt to win him over. But for the rest of the summer he left clay-crusted footprints all over the house and deck.

ALLISON, THE COGNITIVE THERAPIST I'd been seeing once a week since my husband's disappearance, tried to discourage me from going hiking with Jacob. She asked whether I thought I was validating Jacob, buying into his idea that I made his father leave by giving in to Jacob's demands to get out of town, to climb one of Stephen's favorite mountains.

"Going hiking for a few days isn't validation. He wants to go, and I'm taking him," I said, eager for the session to end.

"Think about the process for identifying cognitive errors. Ask yourself, what will this trip accomplish? Is it safe for your son?" What she said made sense. Mt. Scott was one of southern Oregon's smaller peaks, but climbing to the summit would be challenging for an inexperienced hiker with weak lungs like Jacob. She looked at me, waiting for an answer. My eyes roved around her office, landing on the words, *It Is What It Is*, embossed on an inspirational plaque. *Stupid*, I thought. I decided not to come back to her practice again.

AN OBJECT ON THE SIDE of the path caught the sunlight. Jacob, bent on keeping his forward momentum, didn't notice. It was an old two-liter soda bottle. Jacob had insisted we collect any trash we saw along the trail and carry it out with us. But when I picked the bottle up, it jumped in my hand, and I realized there was a small, brownish snake inside. I shrieked and flung it down. Jacob squatted, inspecting the bottle.

"A copperhead," he said, his voice confident. He shook the bottle and the snake thrashed against the plastic, then shot out from the opening and into the woods. Its color was identical to the reddish-brown carpet of pine needles on the forest floor. I could easily have stepped over countless such snakes already during the trip. Crouching on the trail, Jacob stared at the place where the snake had disappeared.

"This is a sign. This means something," he said. This last week, everything had been a sign for Jacob. When he forgot his inhaler at the beginning of the trip it was a sign: it meant he didn't need it anymore. When we lost the trail and had to hike for a full day before finding it again, it was a sign: we should learn to be spontaneous. When he got angry with me for saying that if his father did not come back, we would both be okay eventually, and threw my iPhone—our only phone—into the campfire, he said this was also a sign. It meant I should stop telling lies. His father was gone for good and we would never be okay.

"A sign of what?" I asked, a little sarcastically.

"A sign you should watch where you step." He smiled, and for a minute it felt like things might be all right between us, after all.

We walked on in silence, but when we came over the crest we'd been hiking up, he saw the lake. He dropped his pack with a shout and started running for it. I helplessly watched him struggle down the side of the incline, scrabbling through the brush to get to the water. At the lake's edge he stripped naked, his body a shocking white against the black water. It was late October, too cold to swim. I called after him to stop, but he was already in, striking out toward the lake's center. Soon I could only see his blond head moving farther and farther from the shore. I would check the map later, but I already knew there should not be a lake here, and that we were lost again.

THE YEAR JACOB started high school he had wanted to join the swim team. Stephen encouraged him, probably hoping it could be a turning point—the boy had been an outcast in middle school. But Jacob was not the kind of boy who would do well on a team. He was often withdrawn, sulking into the pages of one of his science fiction books; over the summer he'd read the *Dune* series four times. He mostly avoided eye contact when spoken to, choosing instead to stare at some imaginary point around the speaker's navel. Other times, he could be manic and extroverted, talking too loud and fast about whatever had excited him, pinning his audience with his gaze, his eyes dilated, staring you down. He was difficult to predict. You never knew which version of Jacob would be present on a particular day.

Both Stephen and I had gone with Jacob on the day of the swim tryout, even though we had been suffering through another *bad patch,* as Stephen called them. This was Stephen's phrase for the spans of weeks where we seldom spoke, and he slept in his office in the back of the house. The pool had echoed with the voices of swimmers and parents. Chlorine burned my sinuses. We watched the older kids rip through the water, their tan, muscled bodies making Jacob look even more gangly. Stephen caught my eye, and for a moment I felt like we were really a couple, united by our fear for Jacob, hoping the day would not end in humiliation for him.

Jacob's group was called, and he took off his shirt and smiled at us before lining up at the bottom of the bleachers. The boy standing nearest Jacob stared at the depression in his chest. A girl looked at him and gasped, then nudged her friend and whispered something in her ear. Just before the starting shot, someone said the word *freak.* Jacob's head whipped around. His concentration shattered, and he was last off the blocks. Halfway down the lane, he was in trouble. He choked on a mouthful of water, flailing. The lifeguard had to drag him out of the water, his breath coming in shallow gasps. I grabbed his inhaler from my bag and ran to the edge of the pool. He sucked on the inhaler, and I told him to focus on his breathing, to slow everything down.

Later that night, Stephen would claim that he hadn't heard

anyone say anything, that Jacob had just cracked under pressure. Stephen had chosen not to hear. I had heard it, and so had Jacob.

I ABANDONED MY PACK at the top of the ridge. Moving fast down the incline, I half ran, half slid toward the lake. My hip caught the side of a young pine, knocking me off balance. I put my hands in front of me to break my fall, and pain shot up my right wrist. Turning my hand over to examine the damage, every nerve screamed. My chest heaved and I heard blood rushing in my ears. From my position on the slope, I couldn't see Jacob anymore, so I kept going.

I reached the edge of the water, my wrist already twice its normal size and turning blue. I scanned the surface; the lake was huge. Finally, I saw his head rising and falling between the waves, yellow hair plastered to his skull. He was treading water fifty yards out. I called to him, my voice unfamiliar to me, cracked and broken. Jacob looked in my direction but wouldn't acknowledge me, wouldn't speak or wave. I hated him for it. The mountains rose up around us in all directions. Jacob had been in the lake about twenty minutes, and I considered going in after him. If he had an asthma attack, I would not be able to swim to him in time from the shore. I plunged my wrist into the freezing water, which made the pain worse. Finally, he started to swim back. As he got closer I saw that his lips were blue, and he was breathing hard, moving slow.

Twenty feet from the shore he started choking, looking wild and frightened. I waited on the shore, holding his clothes in one hand, my broken wrist hanging stupid and hot at my side. He stumbled coming out and vomited onto the sand. I'd never seen him completely undressed before. With my good hand, I tried to help him pull his shirt over his head. He looked stronger than I expected, the muscles in his thighs long and tight. The only thing I recognized about him was the hollow depression in his chest. I could have been helping some strange man who had washed ashore, not Jacob. His skin was ice; each breath shook him. I worried about hypothermia. I unbuttoned my flannel shirt and slid it off, bumping my wrist in the process and making my stomach churn with pain. I wrapped the shirt around the tops of his legs and told him to take deep breaths, to slow down. I pressed my body close to his.

I was soaked through, and wind off the lake rushed into my ears. The sun was setting, and soon the temperature would drop. I vowed to never go camping with Jacob again.

•

AFTER JACOB WAS BREATHING NORMALLY, I stood and turned away. With the peak of the crisis over, his nakedness was distracting. Past the sunburned arms, his shoulders were white and smooth, flawless. His light hair was drying, sticking up in a rakish, insolently sexy way. I wanted to look him over, to study him. I shouldn't have to tell him to get dressed, but he just sat there on the sand, staring at the water like an idiot.

"Put your fucking pants on, Jacob," I said. I walked away from him toward the base of the ridge. He could follow me for once. After a minute he caught up, wearing clothes. He was still shaking a little, and he looked again like my son. He eyed my bulging wrist.

"I'll go back up alone. Get our gear," he said. I felt weak, and the ridge looked formidable. Angry as I was with Jacob, I was afraid of being separated from him. He stepped in front of me and put his hands on my shoulders. When he spoke, he sounded completely rational. He talked like someone who wanted to protect me, someone on my side.

"I'll make it back before dark. Promise." I nodded, and he tried to draw me to him, but I made my body rigid and turned away. I wasn't ready to be nice to him just yet. He turned and began to lope up the hill. Even after his attack, his youth gave him a physical advantage in this environment. I could never have kept up with him, even without the injury. Soon he had disappeared in the trees. The waves lapped the shore, rhythmic and uncaring.

TWO YEARS AGO JACOB was prescribed Adderall. He started acting more "normal," making more eye contact, sulking less. He built a large, odd-looking structure behind the house, woven from thin tree limbs and saplings. One afternoon, he came home with a girl, Candy. She was not the kind of girl I would have chosen for him. Silly name, average looks, too much makeup. Jacob brought her into the kitchen to say hello, and she stared at the floor like a cowed animal. She was probably the kind of girl who gave blow jobs to any boy who would let her. Jacob said he wanted to show her his project, and I watched through the kitchen window as the two of them disappeared into the structure. It wasn't long before I heard Candy scream. She came running out with blood pouring from her nose. One pale, fleshy breast flopped free, liberated from her ripped tee-shirt. As she fled down the driveway, Jacob emerged from the shelter, shirtless and calm. He looked at me and smiled—I was sure he could see me staring at him through the window—then turned and went back inside the shelter. I could have told Jacob's father, but I didn't. And I never spoke with Jacob about it, but it was there, our secret, something that held the two of us together. A few days later, Jacob began dismantling the structure as deliberately as he had built it. When he was done there was not a trace of it left. It was like it was never there.

WHEN IT GREW DARK and Jacob had not returned, I began thinking about what must be done to get back home. If we followed the edge of the lake in one direction, we would surely come to a road. Looking at the map, which was in the gear, would help.

As long as I kept my wrist perfectly still, I could almost forget about the injury, but it didn't look good. The blue areas of skin had turned almost black, and my hand was puffing up alarmingly. The stars were coming out when Jacob finally emerged from the forest with our gear. He coughed continuously. He tossed the packs down, and I saw that he had already retrieved my sweater from inside the bag. He probably knew I would have trouble rummaging for it with my injury. We didn't speak as he helped me slide the sweater on over my head. He stretched the cuff of the sleeve out so I could slide my fattened wrist through more easily. I felt my anger toward him soften a little.

"We'll stay here tonight," he said, and started setting up the tent. He laid out our expensive down sleeping bags. We had bought them a week ago, but that day in the camping goods store was a remote memory. He got out the camp stove and started cooking some of the dehydrated beef stew we brought with us. Slow and intent, he seemed focused on caring for us and nothing else. How could he have been so wild just a few hours ago, risking everything by swimming out in the freezing water? Before the lake, I'd hoped as Jacob grew from a boy to a man he would shed his adolescent strangeness, that he would have an adulthood where he was more whole, not more fractured. Now that outcome felt unlikely. I pushed it all aside in exhaustion, grateful that for now, the Jacob I was dealing with was not throwing himself in a lake.

In the tent, I couldn't get my sleeping bag zipped. Jacob offered to do it for me and I let him. We were lying there in the dark, the silence punctuated by his coughs, when he started talking.

"I need to tell you something, Lauren." *Oh god,* I thought. There was only one subject he could possibly want to talk about.

"I know why he left." I kept quiet, hoping he'd lose interest. This was how all of our conversations about Stephen began, and I didn't have the patience to listen to Jacob accuse me, again, of driving his father away.

"I think he found someone else."

"Go to sleep, Jacob."

"You don't want to hear this, but it's true. He had a file on his computer with tons of photos of the same woman in it. Younger than you. Like, twenties." This was the first time Jacob had said anything like this. He was trying to get under my skin, making things up. He moved close to me, the funk from the lake water rising off his skin.

"Before he left he told me. He only married you so he'd have someone to take care of me. He said you were a dead lay."

"Get out of the tent," I said, but I heard the weakness in my voice. I didn't want to be alone with him, in this small dark space with no people for miles around. In one quick movement Jacob shifted his body and was on top of me, pinning me under him in the sleeping bag. His face was inches away from mine, his mouth close enough to kiss or bite me. His rasping, moist breath was sour from the beef stew. His erection pressed into my thigh. *I am not afraid of him*, I told myself over and over. But then he started coughing. He pulled himself off me and turned away, like he was embarrassed by it, the weakness of his lungs. I heard him walk away, but I couldn't be sure how far he'd gone or when he'd come back. My wrist burned, but my fingers had gone numb.

I DON'T REMEMBER FALLING asleep. When I woke up, there was no sign of Jacob. My little finger and ring finger had turned black, and the rest of my hand was mottled, greenish. The wrist was huge. Using my good hand, I searched my pack for the maps, calmly at first and then frantically, but I couldn't find them. I emptied the contents of the bag in the dirt. Nothing. I stuffed my sleeping bag and the rest of the food and water back into my pack. There was no way to break down the tent or pack up the stove with one hand; I left both behind. The long, inky crescent of the lake stretched out on either side of me, identical in either direction. I turned left and started walking along the shore.

THAT NIGHT I LAID out the sleeping bag beside a large rotting log a few yards inside the trees, far enough in to feel hidden but close enough to the water so that I could hear and smell the lake. Sleeping in the tent, I had thought the mountain was quiet, even peaceful. Sleeping outside, the trees were full of noises. Some were recognizable, like the swoosh of a large owl swooping down to capture an unlucky mouse, or the swishing of the wind in higher branches, saying *hush, hush, hush.* But other sounds were undefined and foreign, scurrying, crunching sounds that rustled too close to my sleeping bag. There were far-off low booms that could have no logical explanation.

The night was a physical thing, a cloth pressed to my eyes. I drifted between wakefulness and sleep. There was a dream, an apparition, of someone walking out of the trees and standing a yard away. The sense of a silhouette, faceless and close. The dream repeated, drawing me out of unconsciousness each time to find myself alone and breathing hard in the darkness.

THE NEXT DAY THERE was no sign of Jacob. My wrist was heavy and hot, and the nail fell off my little finger. There were flashes of light at the periphery of my vision, and I told myself this was exhaustion. My body remembered being pinned under Jacob, and I had a physical need to walk, to be moving of my own will. I tried not to think about what he said about the woman. Was he lying? It did not matter, I told myself. I had never thought of Jacob as threatening before—we were always on the same side. I thought of that girl, Candy, who ran from our house two summers ago. I started at every sound—the snapping of a branch, the thud of something falling from a tree. I told myself Jacob was not following me, but how could I be sure? I had been between the expanse of blue-black water on my right and the steep slope on my left for miles, and there was almost no variation in the landscape. Wall of pines on one side, dark water and the incessant waves on the other, speaking the language of insanity. How long could I survive alone here if Jacob never came back, and how would I deal with him if he did?

It was late afternoon when I saw it: a small structure ahead of me. A ranger station, no more than a shack, really, and a road leading away from it, switching back and forth up the incline. The door was closed, the handles circled with thick chain and a padlock. Leaning against the door, the flashes of light pressed at the corners of my vision. A wave of dizziness pulled me downward, and I curled onto the dusty ground in front of the locked entrance.

•

I WOKE UP IN the hospital room. Metal encircled my wrist half-way to the elbow, and I slowly became aware that there were pins going into my arm. A gauze dressing covered my hand. This was Bend, Oregon, I was told, and I had suffered a com-pound fracture in my wrist that cut the blood supply to my lit-tle and ring fingers. The ring finger had nerve damage, and the small finger was amputated. The young doctor who explained this to me was apologetic, his gaze shifting between my face and his polished black shoes.

"Did you find my son?" I asked, and his face got even sorri-er. The two aides in the room glanced at each other nervously.

"My stepson. Jacob. We were on the mountain together," I said.

"No. You were alone." He looked at me with arched eye-brows, not caring to hide his thoughts—*this woman has clearly lost her mind.* When the police came to my hospital room, I told them about Jacob, about how he got into the lake. I told them we had an argument in the tent, about his father. I did not tell them about him climbing on top of me.

•

I HAD BEEN HOME for a month, and there was no sign of Jacob. My arm was still in the cage that held my bones together. The place where my little finger had been continued to throb, and I would have thought it was still attached if I couldn't see the purple stump where the proximal phalange should have been. The rangers who looked for Jacob did not find the tent I left behind or Jacob's pack, and this raised suspicions. A detective was assigned to Jacob's case, a wiry little man with nervous hands. He had a thousand questions. *Could Jacob have located his father? Did I have an idea where Stephen was?* He seemed to find it hard to believe that I could completely lose both a husband and a son within a year's time. *Did Jacob have a girlfriend? Could he be hiding with her?* I told him that it was just the two of us—we were all each other had left. I was advised not to leave town. The detective came back several times, always wanting to talk about the last place I saw Jacob, as if trying to catch me in a lie. I told him it couldn't be my fault he disappeared—how could I ever have really been responsible for someone who was out of my control? I hired an attorney, just in case.

●

THE DAY AFTER JACOB'S eighteenth birthday, I looked through Stephen's computer, for the pictures of the woman Jacob talked about. I found nothing, of course. Just the same files I went through after Stephen disappeared. I walked out behind the house where Jacob's structure used to be, amazed at how both it and he seemed to have been erased. I ran my good hand over the ground and came across a small, unexplained depression in the earth. It was about the width and depth of an apple. I went back inside and bolted the door. Since I made it back from the mountain, I always locked up—even in the daytime. The phone rang that day, and I half expected to answer and hear the voice of a stranger tell me that my son's body had been recovered from a ravine on Mt. Scott, or from the lake, or from some motel room in a town I'd never heard of. At the same time, I half expected it to be Jacob, telling me he was sorry, and he was on his way home.

The Naming of Cats

JENNIFER HAD NEVER THOUGHT much about cats. But once the little beast was purring, black fur glinting under the streetlamp as it rubbed its face against Grace's leg, Jennifer knew she had to get it for her daughter. Jennifer wanted Grace to be happy. Grace was five, and Jennifer only had her for half the week now. Before the cat had appeared, Grace had spent the last two days in a whirling state of want and need, a pint-sized cyclone of demands and directives, shrieks and tears. Now she was sweet, placid even, so the cat was coming home.

They were in a neighborhood park bordered on all sides by brick walk-ups, and the cat was more of a kitten really. Probably it belonged to someone. *Like it matters*, Jennifer thought.

It was close to midnight, and there were dogs, cars, and who knew what else. Even Jennifer, with little or no cat experience, knew the animal wasn't safe outside at night. *People should hang on to the things they want to keep*, she reasoned. To do otherwise was practically to invite someone else to wander in and take whatever he wanted.

"Mommy, he likes me," Grace said. Grace was a solid child, her body geometry falling between pleasingly plump and alarmingly large. At the last well-child visit, the athletic pediatrician had warned—smugly, Jennifer thought—about childhood diabetes. Of course, Jennifer's soon to be ex-wife, Susan, hadn't seen it that way. Susan hadn't noticed the self-righteous gleam in the doctor's eye when he listed the dangers of complex carbohydrates and spikes in blood sugar. She had even suggested Jennifer was interpreting the pediatrician's warning through the filter of a guilty conscience: after all, it was Jennifer who insisted on buying chocolate breakfast cereals—they're delicious!—Jennifer who would not enforce Susan's rule about no extra snacks before bedtime. Susan would probably have advised against taking home a cat from a park, too, if she had been there. The cat arched up in a liquid motion, head-butting Grace's fat little knee, wiping its scent on her, claiming her as its own.

"What about a name?" Jennifer asked.

"Green Grass," Grace said, scratching it under the chin. The cat drooled with pleasure.

"Weird name. You sure?"

"He came out of the grass, and it's green." Jennifer couldn't deny the logic in that. The sound of young, male voices drifted from the other side of the park. She couldn't make out the words at first, but soon she could hear them calling, *here, kitty-kitty-kitty-kitty! Here, Mr. Skittles!*

Their flashlights moved closer, cutting illuminated swaths into the dark grasses and shrubs. Mr. Skittles head-butted Grace's leg again and purred. Jennifer hustled them to the street, pulling Grace along with one hand, swooping up the cat and holding it tight to her chest with the other.

INSIDE THE CAR, THE CAT was different. Grace tried to hold it on her lap. It nipped at her hand and puffed its tail. Grace didn't care. Next, Jennifer tried to hold it while she drove, but it clawed her face, carving a three-inch cut beside her eye, and then wriggled free to squeeze under the passenger seat. Tomorrow, Susan would tell her this was yet another mistake, another thing Jennifer had set in motion without considering the consequences. Jennifer could already hear her. Did it have its shots? What about rabies? But it was too late to change directions. Green Grass yowled like a demon from hell, and Grace giggled, all the way back to Jennifer's almost empty apartment.

By morning it was official: Green Grass was a vector of chaos, a mess-maker extraordinaire. Grace's Dora-the-Explorer comforter was soaked in cat piss, the upholstered chair in her bedroom (where Jennifer had planned to read Grace bedtime stories) was pilled all over with little claw marks, and there was a fresh turd in front of the cheap bi-fold doors to what would be Grace's closet, once the girl had enough clothes and toys to split between the two homes. Jennifer could now see the error of her ways. She would make *Found Cat* signs and plaster the park with them as soon as Grace had been deposited at school. With any luck, Mr. Skittles would be reunited with his rightful owners before the day was over. This she promised herself as she sprayed Lysol on the carpet and cursed the cat under her breath.

"Mommy, he needs a cat box. That's where they poop and pee." Grace slurped the syrupy chocolate-tinted milk from the bottom of her empty cereal bowl, adding, "It's not *his* fault." Grace could be annoyingly perceptive for a five-year-old, Jennifer thought. She poured the last sugary remnants of cereal from the box of Cocoa Puffs into Grace's bowl, then bundled the stinking comforter downstairs to the laundry room.

Getting Grace ready for kindergarten on time had never been easy, and without Susan around to enforce order, they always arrived late on the days Jennifer took her. When they finally got the cat sequestered safely in the bathroom and had walked down the steep concrete stairs of the apartment building, it was clear there was no amount of aggressive driving that would allow Jennifer to make it to the car pool line. This meant she would have to get out of the car in her dingy sweatpants with an oozing cat scratch across her face so she could walk Grace to the gate.

Since the separation, Jennifer had entered a new liminal space with parenting, both publicly and privately. At the beginning of the year, she had loved taking Grace to and from school. Now she dreaded the task, now she felt shamed. She couldn't pretend she was one of those devoted working moms, showing up from some professional endeavor, clean lines pressed into slacks from ankle to groin. It was hard to imagine herself arriving fresh from a run, taut tan calves exposed, flexing their tan superiority at all the soft, gently pudgy stay-at-home mothers lined up to collect their broods.

Not that she had ever been either of those types of women. Jennifer did not like to exercise, and her online job processing Census data did not require her to dress for success, or even to get dressed at all, if she didn't care to. She often arrived on the scene with a slouch, walking with tenderness to the gate to pick up her little girl so as not to disturb a hangover. But she was there, she was doing it, this parenting thing, and she was a woman who was married to a woman, and this had made her a kind of rock star among the hens. They had smiled at her, before. Now, most of them wouldn't even glance her way.

ONE OF THE FEW mothers who didn't avoid eye contact, Kim Schaffer, always appeared at the school looking like she had just rolled out of some glamorous bed. Her look was simple but compelling: a dusting of iridescent eye shadow, no bra, and small, pointed breasts that Jennifer had always thought would fit perfectly in her mouth. This morning Kim was arriving late as well—she walked up to the gate just after Grace had bounded away toward her class. Kim had her twin girls in tow, Grace's friend, and the other girl, who was always indistinct in Jennifer's mind—children who were not of interest to her daughter were subsequently of no interest to her.

Jennifer noticed that Kim was pregnant again. She had all the puffiness of the second trimester about her, and she reminded Jennifer of the way Susan had looked before Grace was born—filled with the simple joy of blithe, maternal sexuality. Just seeing Kim like that made Jennifer feel pulled backward, like she could pretend that she and Susan were still in the stage of rapt possibility, still ignorant of how much of each other they were about to lose to their daughter.

"Ouch," Kim said, nodding at the scratch beside Jennifer's eye.

"We kind of adopted a cat last night. From the park."

"Kind of?" Kim's eyes narrowed, and Jennifer knew she'd said the wrong thing, as she often did around the other parents. Kim was already cocking her head to the side, looking out of the corner of her eye for someone else to talk to. Jennifer quickly explained how the cat had walked up out of the grass, no collar, nobody in sight, and had made Grace so happy that she couldn't bear to separate them. She left out the part about the boys calling for Mr. Skittles; it was almost irrelevant.

"It was the first time she'd smiled. She hardly smiles anymore, you know? Since Susan and I have been un-coupling."

At the mention of un-coupling, Kim's face twisted a little.

"I heard. But. I'm sorry?" This was how it always went.

Faltering condolences, awkward pauses. The topic of the breakup made their mutual friends and acquaintances uncomfortable, and no matter how much she tried to make un-coupling sound healthy and holistic, like a spirulina smoothie or a kale-chip salad, everyone knew it sucked.

"I'm okay. Really. It's Grace that's important."

Kim's face un-scrunched, and Jennifer could feel herself being reconsidered, reinvented in Kim's eyes: the self-sacrificing, separated mother, enduring lacerations, sleepless nights, and cat-pee-soaked blankets to please her little girl. Maybe the cat wasn't such a bad idea after all. Still, she was determined to undo what she had done, to make the flyers, to return the cat. What had she been thinking? After all—Mr. Skittles belonged to somebody. The cat should be reunited with its owners so it could work on destroying their house instead. Grace would understand. She was a smart kid. She was resilient.

STOPPING AT A COPY SHOP, she used a marker to write a simple sign. *Cat. Found. Call to Identify.* She ran twenty copies, bought a stapler, and headed back to the scene of the crime. The park was less mysterious in the daytime, and it didn't look like a place where anybody could find anything of value. Why did she persist in bringing Grace here? The tall grass was more brown than green, straw yellow in places and choked with cinders of thistle and bits of discarded plastic. The play structures were worn and marked with a palimpsest of graffiti, and one side of the plastic slide had been melted and charred, perhaps by fireworks, perhaps by a simple act of malice and lighter fluid. Jennifer struggled to staple the flyers to the trunks of failing pear trees that had been planted on the borders of the park, most likely in good faith. But they were faltering without the regular pruning and watering they needed. The voice that spoke was startlingly close by, and the words slipped around her, greasy and thick.

"Cat done messed you up. Scratched that pretty face all to shit." The homeless man had a reek of urine and something indeterminate but foul about him, and his dark face was gnarled around a collection of teeth that seemed to come from different mouths.

"Got a cigarette?" He stepped closer, and Jennifer noticed how wiry he was, the flexing tendons in his forearms, the veins like wires or worms wrapping around the muscle under mottled skin. She was ashamed to think of him as grotesque, but she couldn't shake the thought that being touched by him would be the worst thing imaginable.

"I don't." Jennifer turned and began back to the car. Why would her body not obey her command to be fearless—sweating palms, color rushing to her face—why could she not make herself unafraid? She was an adult, after all—a mother, even! Surely this person was harmless; deranged and unlucky, certainly, but harmless.

"You still nice to look at. But it gonna be there," he oiled on, clicking his tongue lasciviously behind chapped and seeping lips, nodding at her wound as he followed along, surprisingly light on his feet and close behind. "Gonna leave a scar," he said, sounding like he knew what he was talking about.

Jennifer shut and locked the car door, thinking, *classic white-lady shit, that's what I'm doing.* The man slapped his grimy hand on the driver's side window, smacking the glass right by Jennifer's face, palm swelling against the clear barrier, a sore in the center of his hand opening like a mouth. When she pulled the car away, his handprint remained, a smear of oil and pinkish fluid from the wound. She looked back at the man, swaying on the sidewalk in her rearview. He raised his ragged hand in a parting gesture, and Jennifer couldn't decide if she wished she could help him, or if she wanted him and all forlorn people like him wiped from the face of the earth.

●

THERE WAS A GAS station at the grocery where she planned to pick up cat supplies—who knew if the owners would even see her sign—and Jennifer dipped the squeegee into the dark blue fluid and set about erasing the handprint from her window. It took pressure and effort, and the water ran brackish down the handle of the squeegee onto her wrist. In the cavernous fluorescent aisles of the store the other shoppers kept their distance, and Jennifer could feel her own eyes looking at people the wrong way. There was something of that lunatic in the park about her. She knew because these moods had gripped her throughout her life. That was why he'd approached her, sniffed her out—he'd sensed one of his own kind. The cut on her face burned and itched, and she felt the familiar descent as she tumbled down into herself, becoming less and less able to make sense of the smallest social interactions. Hurriedly, she beeped her items through the U-scan, hoping to avoid any unnecessary contact.

When she returned to her apartment bearing her gifts—cat food, litter, catnip mouse—Jennifer found that Green Grass had escaped the bathroom and clawed down the cheap miniblinds in the living room. He sat in the middle of the floor, switching his tail back and forth in defiance. Jennifer saw that the cat was not really black at all. Why had she not noticed this before? In the park at night it had been dark, too dark to see many details, but she'd gotten a pretty close look at him when she stuffed him into the tiny bathroom with the plastic shower stall and the fluorescent lights a few hours ago. Instead of flat black, in the sunlight the cat's fur was in fact a deep charcoal color with subtle swirls of the darkest brown stripes patterning its undercoat, giving it an exotic appearance. Was the cat somehow being transformed, perhaps by the adoration of her child? Jennifer dismissed the thought as crazy—more lunatic-in-the-park think. And yet, there was something empty and wretched about the apartment that the cat seemed almost miraculously to fix. The place felt more alive with him sauntering about. The cheap blinds he had destroyed had been making her feel even worse, Jennifer realized, and without them the room looked better. There was even an inviting splash of sunshine on the worn leather sofa—the one Susan had wanted to donate just last year—making it look appealing and warm.

Collapsing into that pool of brightness on cracked, tanned leather made Jennifer weak with relief, and she allowed herself to sigh audibly. In no time, the cat was on top of her. It licked her ears raw with its spiked tongue, it purred as it massaged her chest with its paws. Staring hypnotically into her eyes, the cat seemed to know her, to need her. *You are deserving of love*, she seemed to hear the cat say, and although she knew it was her imagination speaking to her, Jennifer wondered if her imagination would have been so moved, without the cat. She thought not. As she drifted in that trance, in that undecided space between fantasy and sleep, she became vaguely aware that she had forgotten to buy any cereal at the store, or anything to feed Grace for dinner that night.

They could find food at Susan's.

JENNIFER STILL HAD A KEY to their old house, the Arts and Crafts with all of the embellishments that Jennifer adored and Susan had thought unnecessarily fussy. Susan had said it was important they have access to each other's homes; it was part of the holistic un-coupling plan that they would continue to share some co-habitational space. After all, Susan had said, it was best for the child. But Susan had never used her key to enter Jennifer's new place.

After assuring Grace that Green Grass was safe and sound back at her apartment, and that he would still be there when they went back later that night, Jennifer plopped the girl down in front of the TV with *The Lion King* and a microwaved "healthy" kids' macaroni dinner from the well-stocked freezer. Now she was free. If Jennifer timed it right, she could have a leisurely soak in the tub while the movie played, and then bundle Grace back to her apartment before Susan came home. Her wife had always worked late—as long as Jennifer cleared out by seven-thirty there was almost no chance of an accidental encounter.

In the bath, Jennifer felt both relaxed and reinvigorated. It was a large claw-foot tub, in a bigger and nicer bathroom than she could ever have afforded on her own, and she half-floated in its womb-like center, thinking about nothing much and reading descriptions of cat breeds on her phone.

The names of cats, which she'd never before paid much attention to, sounded musical, magical even. Abyssinian, Balinese, Bengal, Chartreux. The bath was a good place to get reacquainted with one's body, she thought, and noticed that her belly had developed a pleasing extra layer of fat on it since she had moved out. Not too much, but just enough to support her as she leaned forward to refill her wine glass. She was considering turning on the faucet and letting it splash vigorously between her legs, perhaps while playing a mental slideshow of pregnant Kim and pregnant Susan-of-the-past, when she heard Susan's key in the lock and knew that she would instead soon have to speak, soon have to engage in another pointless conversation with Susan-of-the-present.

Susan stood in the doorway, framed in steam rising from the tub. There was a pushing, physical desire in Jennifer's throat to speak about the cat. But she felt that speaking about the animal and its story would cheapen the whole thing somehow, rob the tale of its power, and make it like everything else, random, stupid and meaningless. *A crazy person followed me to my car today. I went to the store and forgot to get Cocoa Puffs. I think I am falling in love with a cat.* Was it like this for every couple? Did marriage and children always make a person realize just how alone we are in the universe?

"Could've told me. That you'd be here. In the tub." Susan had a look, but what did the look mean? That she wanted Jennifer out, or that she wanted to be invited in? Either could lead to a fight.

"Come in. If you want," Jennifer said, wishing Susan would not want to. Susan started unbuttoning and peeling off layers without ceremony or seduction. Jennifer lingered on Susan's taut abdominals. The firmness of her wife's midsection seemed like a criticism, like Susan had been hitting the gym a few extra times this last month, just so she could prove how much better off she was without Jennifer. But Susan had always been athletic. Just months after Grace was born, she looked like she had never even been pregnant—people often assumed it was Jennifer who had given birth to the baby.

Slipping into the bath, Susan winced at the temperature.

"Are you going to tell me? What happened to your face."

"Maybe later."

"Don't worry about running out the water tank. Not like you have to pay for it." Susan tried to lift the words up at the end with a laugh, like she didn't mean to be cruel.

"Right. I'm not paying."

BACK AT THE APARTMENT that night, Grace tried to win Green Grass's affection, but he flitted away from her pudgy, outstretched hands. He ignored her calls of *here, kitty-kitty*, and the more Grace stamped her foot the less Green Grass deigned to be near her. Instead, the cat rubbed the side of his face against Jennifer's leg. Grace finally gave up the chase and retreated to her bed.

"You made him like you. He loves you better than me," Grace said, peering from under the covers. Jennifer climbed into bed with her little girl. The child radiated a kind of sullen heat, and being under the blanket with her was too much.

Jennifer adjusted the covers so that her legs were exposed, and Green Grass jumped up onto her lap, purring.

"Green Grass is supposed to be mine," said Grace, her voice rising on *mine* with a kind of desperation, Jennifer thought, as if the child already understood the futility of that word.

"And he is. It's okay for him to like me too, right?" Jennifer asked, scratching the cat under its chin. *Please,* Jennifer thought to the cat. *Please be good to Gracey. Just give her something.*

Green Grass arched his back, curving his long and sinuous spine into a sideways letter C, and placed one paw tentatively on Grace's warm lap. The child seemed to almost stop breathing. The cat began to knead its paws methodically. Grace, who had always fought sleep like it was death itself, began to breathe in rhythm with Green Grass's purr. Jennifer sat as still as she could, and in a few minutes her daughter's eyes flickered closed, and she was asleep.

"Thank you," she whispered, feeling only a little ridiculous for talking to the cat. When she left the room and went to her own bed, the cat followed.

THE NEXT MORNING THE FIGHT with Grace started over nothing, as usual. Or almost nothing. First, Grace had woken up early

149

and, upon discovering Green Grass in Jennifer's bed, she had picked up the cat and flung him rudely to the floor. The cat had retreated, hissing and spitting under Jennifer's dresser, where he seemed determined to stay until Grace was gone.

Next, Grace discovered there was no more chocolate cereal. She said she'd rather starve than eat bran flakes. Grace would not get dressed and would not brush her teeth on her own. By the time Jennifer had wrestled Grace into a sweatshirt dress and the almost-too-small leggings Susan had insisted on packing for her and had forcibly brushed Grace's teeth, the girl's round face was puffed from screaming. Her howls ran from long and guttural to shrill and earsplitting as Jennifer begged and threatened, shouted and sweet-talked.

Grace began to chant, *I hate you I hate you I hate you,* over and over through her sobs. Jennifer fought the urge to strike her, or choke her into silence, but of course she never would, never could, harm her little girl. Besides, it would give Susan too much satisfaction—prove her right about Jennifer's lack of maternal ability. She picked Grace up as roughly as she dared, flipped her squirming body upside down and carried her, wailing, down the common stairs in the apartment building.

How had it come to this? One part of her mind was watching from some more rational place, the rest of her was powerless before the storm surge of rage that pushed them both forward. How was it that she was tied to this merciless little girl, her daughter, who would not obey her and who would not stop screaming? Jennifer had just stuffed her unceremoniously into her car seat and restrained her in the five-point harness when Grace emitted a guttural snarl and bit Jennifer's wrist with a decisiveness that surprised them both. Grace stopped screaming and stared, sniffling, but unafraid. Jennifer rubbed her arm and smelled the blood, high and metallic, before she saw it, both on Grace's chin and dripping down her own hand, onto the pavement.

Jennifer pulled up to the school right on time. There was no danger of missing the car pool line this time. After Grace got out of the car, Jennifer folded up the blue fleece blanket that she wrapped around Grace's lap when it was chilly, then set it neatly to the side of the car seat. It was the blanket that she and Susan had used most often to tuck her into her infant carrier and stroller, and it had a small, friendly-looking dolphin splashing through some embroidered waves on one corner. Jennifer had the urge—irrational, she knew—to refold the little blanket so that the dolphin was on the outside, so that her daughter might see it when she next picked her up from school. For what reason, Jennifer thought—to let her know that she was loved, to make her feel safe?

Could any of the paraphernalia of infancy or child-hood really make up for the fact that although she loved her daughter, she often could not stand to be near her? She hated the way these sentimental thoughts made her mouth dry up and her stomach feel as though it was folding over on itself, like her body and mind were working in concert, conspiring to add to her misery. All of this was the kind of thinking Jennifer knew she should not share with Susan; it could probably be used later as evidence.

The phone, having been left behind in haste or fury or both, was vibrating on the counter when she returned to the apartment. A message on the phone, a woman's voice, soft and childlike: *Hi, this is Angie, and um, I think you found my cat? He looks black, but, he actually has some, like, stripes? My boys have been going crazy looking for him. Let me know, okay, and oh, thank you!* Jennifer felt a swish of sable fur between her ankles and registered the throb of Green Grass's baritone purr against her skin. She looked at the voicemail on her phone and pressed delete.

It was done. She picked Green Grass up and took him to the sofa with her. They snuggled into their spot, and Jennifer caressed him, traced his stripes with her fingertips and thought intently about the lifespan of cats. Surely they had years and years ahead of them together. She wanted Susan to see him now, now that it was official. She would ask Susan to come over that night, she decided. They would all be together, and surely, Susan would be charmed by the cat, too. After all, who could resist such a magical beast?

HAVING SUSAN AT THE APARTMENT made it feel as though things were shifting into a new, perhaps more normal way of doing things together for Grace. When Jennifer had asked Susan to come over for a family dinner, she'd heard Susan's sharp inhalation over the phone, the quick little breath her wife always took before politely refusing Jennifer's invitations. But then, Susan had taken another breath. "Well," she'd said, "I would like to get a look at this cat."

Neither Grace nor Jennifer mentioned their dust up, and with a Band-Aid covering the crescent moon shaped bite mark on Jennifer's wrist, it seemed the matter was closed. After dinner, Susan made popcorn on the stove with garlic and sea salt, and Green Grass licked the salt from Susan's fingertips, "What a beautiful cat, how lucky that you found him," she said, as they watched some inane children's show on Netflix.

Susan helped Grace into her pajamas and supervised the brushing of teeth. Susan tucked her into bed, shut the door three quarters of the way just like she always did at their real home, and read her to sleep while Jennifer cleaned up the dinner table.

When Susan came out of the bedroom, Jennifer felt the sickening need, the nauseating desire to tell her about the deleted phone message, the awful car ride to school that morning. Could Susan feel it? Could she smell the longing emanating from Jennifer like malodorous perspiration? Susan sat down next to her on the parched old sofa and wrapped her strong, lean fingers through Jennifer's shorter digits.

"I want you to stop coming back to the house," Susan said. "It's too hard on her. And me." Jennifer nodded, and Susan looked away. Perhaps being with someone, truly together, was more terrifying than having that chasm to yell across, Jennifer thought. Perhaps things were more bearable when one didn't have all the details. The house keys came off their rings without a fight, and Jennifer pressed hers into Susan's palm without a show, without a gesture that would let either of them acknowledge everything it meant, or everything it didn't mean.

Once the door had shut and she heard Susan's car pull out of the parking lot, Jennifer slipped into Grace's darkened bedroom. The child's breath churned rhythmic and warm as she sat down next to her on the bed. From beside the tangle of Grace's brown hair on the pillow, the cat peered up at Jennifer. Green Grass was kneading Grace's hair with its white claws, purring, keeping Grace subdued even as she slept. At that moment Jennifer had never felt more affection for another animal; he was possibly the most beautiful creature she had ever seen.

His eyes were a deep emerald, his coat was short and dense like the velvety pelt of a creature from a fairytale, a mythical beast imbued with ineffable powers. His whiskers were unusually long and curved, and a second set of whiskers fanned out from above the cat's eyes, framing its face like elegant tendrils. *Mister Skittles*, Jennifer thought. It was a ridiculous name. Such a cat deserved better. Why must people name animals without any regard to the dignity of their souls? She smiled to herself, because that was just the kind of thing she would often say to Susan that would cause Susan to look at her strangely, making Jennifer feel it would have been better not to say anything out loud. She thought, for the first time in years, of a T.S. Eliot poem she had loved as a child, "The Naming of Cats."

She could not remember the poem word for word, but there was one thing of which she was sure: the poet had stipulated that cats must have not one, not two, but three different names. The first name, Jennifer remembered, should be common, a name for everyday use. *Mr. Skittles* might actually be serviceable in this regard. But the second name should be more elegant and sophisticated, something a cat could take pride in—*Green Grass* could certainly serve as such a moniker. But what of the third name? A quick search on her phone brought up the whole poem, and there in the dark beside her daughter, her new cat kneading her lap in the blue glow of the phone's screen, Jennifer read the last stanza over and over like an incantation.

> *But above and beyond there's still one name left over,*
> *And that is the name that you never will guess;*
> *The name that no human research can discover—*
> *But the cat himself knows, and will never confess.*

The words gentled her thoughts, tumbled in her mind, smoothing off the sharp edges of her sadness until she was calm enough to begin purring herself. If only she could have three names as well, Jennifer thought, one for her daughter, one for her wife, and one for herself. What could be wrong with that?

"What's your *real* name," she whispered to the cat. She

could try to guess it, but it would not seem right—to impose something so personal on a unique, free thing like Mr. Skittles Green Grass. Jennifer and her cat were right for each other, and she knew it with a certainty that left no room for guilt over something as trivial as cat-snatching. She had no concern that he would have been better off with his previous owners— they would never really have understood him—not the way she did. Green Grass deserved better, and Jennifer never doubted it.

EVEN AFTER THE PAPERS were signed and the divorce was final, even when Grace grew into a teenager and refused to speak to her, Green Grass was there with Jennifer. Season after season, he continued to watch her with his jeweled eyes, purring, presenting his regal head for petting. He was the best mistake Jennifer had ever made.

MEGAFAUNA

THE WORST PART about cleaning the goat skins was the smell, a copper blood stink that stayed on Adah's hands long after she had rooted out the congealed, purple grime from underneath her fingernails with a sharpened twig. Livestock was rare in the Jungle, and how the goats had arrived was a mystery to Adah. She would probably never know how the animals had been brought in or who would eat them because nobody told her anything, ever. Adah was considered doubly cursed because she was both female and mute. Her tongue had somehow failed to develop into a muscle capable of producing language. She could eat and drink like everyone else, but the rogue muscle disobediently flopped in her mouth whenever she attempted to speak. Delinquent and defiant, it refused to shape her breath into anything other than *Uuuhh, Uuuhh* sounds. Jahid, who was the de facto leader of the camp's contingent from her country because he had been in the Jungle the longest and had attempted the most crossings, led Adah to a patch of bloodied ground where the goats had been slaughtered and skinned. He handed her a rough blade and said, "nazif," *clean*. Adah did not refuse.

THE SMELL OF GOAT DUNG didn't bother Adah. The pebbles of recently digested grass, caked now in the grooves of her feet, seemed somehow cleaner than the blood, perhaps because the smell of live goats reminded her of her village. But the odor of blood always meant death was near, or at least shame. Still, she scraped the skins, discarding the bits of fat too rank to consider eating into an oily pile in the dirt, then placed the cleaned skins in a tub of soaped water where they slid under the still surface and rested, opalescent pink side up and hairy side down. A long femur had been tossed in with the skins, and Adah rent it down the middle with her blade. Bringing the bone to her mouth, she sucked out the marrow and lipped the fat from the groove of the bone.

With the hides scraped and the marrow sucked, Adah looked for Jahid. Even in the heaving sea of desperate people he was easy to spot. Jahid carried himself like someone important. He had a way of always standing with one hip pushed cockily out to the side with his ankles crossed, his chin tilted up toward the heavens as if he was waiting for some intervention from above, like he was tuned in to the invisible currents of life that assured him he would make it, he would cross to the UK and be free. He leaned against the one scrubby tree in front of the endless shantytown that was the Jungle, a tent city of blue and silver tarps and little hovels made from packing crates. A thick cloud of smoke from hundreds of small cooking fires was hanging like fog between the muddy ground and the gray sky, and Adah thought it was the ugliest place she had ever seen. She placed herself in front of Jahid and handed him the blade to indicate that she had finished. He looked at her like she was a riddle to be solved by someone else. "Ib'd," he said, *go away.*

Adah joined the line of other unaccompanied youths who shuffled toward a tent set up by one of the NGOs. She had just turned fifteen but looked younger than her age so nobody questioned her when she queued up for the extras given to children, although she had seen some turned away for looking too old. Having arrived only a few days ago during a mid-July downpour that had turned the dirt roads in the camp to muddy tracts stretching in all directions, Adah knew none of the others. In front of her in line was a girl with milk-fogged, glassy eyes who batted at the flies that worried an infected gash across her face; the flies wanted the yellowish fluid that ran down her cheeks in rivulets and crusted at her collarbone. The girl wore a faded yellow T-shirt that said Hollywood, California, USA, in flowing cursive writing. Adah moved with the line swaying slightly in the heat. She looked down instead of looking into the faces of the others, preferring to be alone. She counted the flies that circled the ankles of the afflicted girl in front of her, by fives. Five. Ten. Fifteen. Twenty. Then the ankles were gone, and the boy behind her gave her a push, not too hard, to let her know she had reached the front. There, a woman poured a small package of powder into a plastic cup filled with water and motioned for Adah to drink.

When Adah lifted the cup to her mouth, the odor of blood from her fingernails caught in her nostrils, and the marrow rose in her throat. She dropped the cup, spilling the water that must have been mixed with medicine or something precious, and the woman scowled and cursed her in French, a language she didn't understand. The woman, whose hands were huge, seemed to want Adah to explain herself, and when Adah opened her mouth and made her utterances, so clearly non-sense in any language, the woman pulled her from the line and into the Médecins Sans Frontières tent.

In the tent, a doctor was tending a boy whose left foot was missing, his leg terminating in a surprisingly smooth stump above where his ankle would have been.

"Is there pain?" the doctor asked, his Arabic clumsy. The boy squinted his eyes tightly as if his suffering was intense and shook his head vigorously in reply. Adah knew to be skeptical. Her uncle had also lost a foot, severed in the distant past, and she had never seen him complain of pain. This boy's wound was completely healed—how could it possibly trouble him so? Her uncle had been cruel to his wife and even to his horse; Adah had seen him strike both woman and animal as though there were no difference between the two. She had a reflex-ive dislike of most amputees, and she had observed that such people often thought their injury entitled them to more. The woman who had brought her to the tent had her sit on a metal stool under a gently swinging light. The woman walked over to the doctor, speaking one French word that sounded familiar to Adah, since it was what most of the aid workers had said about her: *Mute.* When Adah caught the boy's eye over the humped shoulder of the doctor, he winked at her.

The doctor directed the boy to lie on a cot and went to Adah. He was the cleanest man she had ever seen in a camp, and his face was thin and long. For a European, he was pretty to look at. His eyes were light green, almost yellow, and his lips had a fullness that was unexpected. He introduced himself as Lalande, and when he asked in halting Arabic if she understood English, she nodded. Lalande spoke English in a way she liked, almost a monotone without any detectable accent. Lalande gripped Adah's chin and turned her face this way and that; his fingertips with the nails trimmed down to nothing lingered on her skin for too long. His touch made her feel seasick, like all the water inside her was rocking back and forth, and when he took his hand away she was relieved.

Lalande was perfunctory but not cold, and he was probably at least forty, but with them, it was hard to tell.

"Open your mouth," he said. He put on a white plastic glove and swept two fingers under her tongue, pressing hard into the place it was rooted to the floor of her mouth. His mouth twitched, and he almost seemed to smile.

"I know at least five surgeons who could repair this easily," he said, pulling his sheathed fingers from her mouth. When Lalande took the glove off, Adah saw there was one place on his body that appeared dark and stained. The skin of his right thumb and index finger was a tawny brown color and his fingernails were yellow. Perhaps because he noticed her gaze on his blemished fingers, he put his hand inside his pants pocket.

"Can you write your name for me?" he asked and produced a black pen and small book from his pocket. The book was bound in green leather, and it seemed out of place in the camp—a ridiculous luxury. The dark ink flowed from the pen onto the page as Adah wrote. In the fluorescent light of the tent, her name reverberated, and it seemed like a secret contract between them. Adah knew that this unlikely doctor wanted to be her friend.

ADAH HAD KILLED HER PARENTS by being born. Most of the girls at the camp had neither a mother nor father to cleave to, and if their parents were still living, they were unreachable. But Adah knew that she was complicit in her parents' deaths in a way the others weren't. Her own mother's life had been wrung from her by the act of giving birth. Her Aunt Maia had told Adah of the blood that came after labor—unstoppable and unceasing, saturating the mattress just two hours after Adah had been born. Baby Adah's suckling mouth had had to be forced open with a spoon and pried from her mother's breast, which grew cold and could not release the milk that her tiny mouth sought.

Adah had killed her father more slowly. He was a man with a face that always looked inward, Adah had thought, a face that wanted to fold itself away into nothing. He rarely spoke to her. When she was seven years old he tried to hitch a ride on a passing train. Had he hoped to escape his mute child who had taken his wife from him? Adah wondered. Everyone in town said her father's hands must have slipped from the oiled rung on the side of the train, the relentless momentum slinging him beneath its great mass, thundering on and nothing but blood and bone left on the track. How could he have been so foolish? They whispered in town. Surely he knew that the train, which passed through just once a week, would be moving too fast, they said, some quietly and others in loud shrill voices.

Whether by accident or design, Adah's father was dead, and tradition had required that the eldest child go to the place of a father's death and publicly mourn. Adah was placed in the care of her one-footed uncle, and he haltingly walked her to the tracks, leaning on the old prosthetic that had been pigmented the color of milk mixed with blood, clearly created for use by a white person. His creased, rocklike hand tried to hold hers in a comforting way and tried not to squeeze too tight or to drag her along. Adah had been sure that his hand, at least, meant well. The smear and gristle on the tracks that had been her father did not look like a man at all. It looked like an erasure of a person perhaps, but there was no person there to mourn. Sadness seemed impossible. A crowd began forming around them, and people whispered about this strange, silent girl who was not screaming and tearing her hair in terror, like a good, respectful child would. Her uncle's hand tightened around hers, and the people squinted, waiting. Moaning as best she could, Adah pressed her face to her uncle's trousers and hid her tearless eyes. She felt her uncle's body relax, and he stroked her hair like she was a small, fragile creature, now that she had saved them by doing what was expected. If she ever tried to catch a train she would not fall off, she thought. It would take more than a thousand tons of steel to erase her from the earth.

That night her uncle's wife Maia had brought her to their tents, and Adah was shown to her new sleeping place, a woven grass mat on the dirt floor of the kitchen. She felt that this place, her uncle's home, wanted to rub her away into the dust. She vowed to leave it, when she could. Her father's life had been the only thread tethering her to this village, to these people, and without him, she was free to plan a new life for herself. She now owed this place nothing, not the lank tents with their dim and smoky interiors, not the gritty yards pungent with goat dung, not the sandy, rocky path to the well with its obsidian black circle of water and metal pail splashing down like the moon falling from the sky into the only cool place in the village. After her father's death, Adah belonged only to herself. This had been her inheritance, his one and only gift to her.

WHEN LALANDE SPOKE her name, his voice quavered and tripped, lifting the ending syllable up into the air where it wobbled. Still, he liked to say her name and she liked to hear it spoken because it made her know that she was still alive. Having her name put on a list seemed to prove this more than the bones in her face and the weight of her own swollen tongue, curled in her mouth and waiting for some metamorphosis that would allow her to speak.

Lalande wore a dark indigo cotton shirt and smoked Dunhill cigarettes incessantly in the medic tent. Adah liked the smell. She lingered in the tent with him. He gave her cigarettes that she would never smoke—they were more precious than gold in the Jungle and could be traded for essentials like toilet paper and toothpaste. Lalande read to her from the cigarette packages about how smoking would clog your arteries and cause cancer. Adah laughed, which for her was a kind of grunt; what a luxury it must be to die of smoking too many of those precious little packaged sticks of tobacco, and not from trains or sickness or from lack of love. Lalande looked at her with puzzlement but smiled, the corner of his mouth twitching as his gold-green eyes roved over her face.

After that meeting, he liked to read to her in English in the medic tent, and he told her things that seemed to matter, bringing a new magazine to read to her whenever he returned from outside, from Calais. The magazines were always issues of *National Geographic* and told stories of almost unbelievable places like Seoul, in South Korea, where everyone had a cell phone and girls Adah's age had surgeries on their faces to make them look like Caucasians—if you had the money, you could buy yourself an eyelid crease. A lean, French nose could be yours for the taking, if you could pay enough.

CALAIS WAS THE FRENCH city that bordered the Jungle, and it was a magical place. Adah learned this and more from the one-footed boy, whose name was Matteau. Matteau was forever at the

medic tent, and when Adah gave him one of the precious cigarettes Lalande had shared with her, Matteau started talking
and it seemed he would never stop. In Calais, he said, there
was a mighty tunnel under the English Channel that led to
England and real doctors and schools and freedom. The Brit-
ish welcomed all migrants and gave them apartments and a
stipend and medical care and education, and it was almost
always sunny and the streets always shimmered like mirag-
es in the desert because of the strength of the sunlight. The
problem was that the English would not take migrant travelers
from France without papers, and one had to be able to claim
a family member there to gain asylum. "But do not worry,"
said Matteau, "There is always work for a pretty girl like you.
No papers, no problem," he grinned, and Adah knew it meant
something nasty, what he said, but she did not care.

One could, according to Matteau, catch a ride on or under
a lorry, or even on the top of one of the passenger trains that
zoomed through the tunnel, taking rich Europeans back and
forth seven times a day. *Le Shuttle* trains carried everything
the ferries did—passengers, cars, freight, and it took only
thirty-five minutes, according to Matteau. But many died this
way, he said, and escaping the camp itself first was no easy
task. Adah had seen the lines of young French police with

their strong jaws and gleaming, well-oiled automatic weapons, ready to strike down any brown person who might try to seep out into their shining city by the sea. Their body armor had glistened in the rain as Adah passed them on her way into the Jungle. From the van window Adah saw that they wore boots so fine that they must be protected from the filth of the camp by plastic covers that looked like clear shopping bags. They caught the light and crinkled like the cellophane used to wrap the fresh cut flowers that rich people bought to decorate their dinner tables. Calais must be worth protecting at any cost, Adah thought, for such men to be away from their loving homes and blonde wives and children, day and night, just to keep people like her inside.

THE NIGHT BEFORE THE FIGHTING had finally come to her village, Adah had seen her uncle with Maia naked and straddling him in their tent. At first, she saw only the legs of her uncle, all rope and sinew, toes pointed on his remaining foot, stump of the other missing leg unwrapped and quivering under the round milky folds of Maia's body. Then Maia had turned and lolled her dark sad eyes to where Adah stood in the doorway. Uncovered, her hair was ugly and coarse, Adah thought, not

smooth like her mother's had been in the one photograph
Adah owned of her. Although she knew she ought to feel embarrassed to judge a woman who had the misfortune to be
married to her uncle, Adah was repelled by her aunt's rolling
body, her thick hair. The limp jiggle of Maia's lip and the perspiration on her forehead all spoke of surrender, and surrender to this man at that. Heat pressed across Adah's face like a
hand. This would not be her life, she had decided as she pulled
the curtain back across the doorway and walked out into the
night. She could not let herself be married in the village, and
she knew that if she stayed her uncle would want to find a husband to take her soon. Word of the war came the next day, and
Adah left the following morning. Barefoot, she walked alone
into the purple, predawn light. She took only herself, leaving
everything behind except the small wooden cross necklace
Aunt Maia had given her and the sacred photograph of her
own mother, tucked between the pages of her useless pock-
et-sized black Bible, for protection.

Adah's uncle and his family were Christians, and Adah en-
joyed the ritual of prayer, even though she knew God didn't
exist. When she looked up at the stars she knew they were
swirled together of stuff grander than the meager human
imaginings of Christ, and that the universe was held together

by gravity, not the Son of God made flesh. Many ridiculous ideas about creation were recorded in scripture. She knew, because she had learned to read English by reading the pocket Bible. But still she had liked to pray while she lived in the village. She was never disturbed or made to draw water from the well when she knelt soundlessly praying in the kitchen that was her bedroom, as motes of dust became golden stardust floating in the late afternoon sun. Adah liked the cross Maia had given her as well because it looked like an intersection to her, and she came to think its four directional spokes reached out to the cardinal directions to show that all paths could be open to her.

IN THE TENT at Girl's Camp there were at least fifty girls just like Adah, each one the same because she had lost everything but each unique in her own anguish. Bony hip to pointed raw pelvis, they lay tightly packed across the floor of the tarped enclosure at night. After she had kept coming to the medic tent every day for a month, Lalande had asked her where she slept. When she shrugged her shoulders—she had not yet been able to trade anything for a tent of her own, she usually slept in the scrub brush behind the UNCHR food distribution tent—

he said he was taking her to a place called the Girl's Camp. It was a half mile walk from Lalande's station to Girl's Camp, and he had to remain stone-faced as he led Adah there by the elbow. Adah had never seen him like this. He refused to give any of the boys who approached him anything, and his only words were stern and in a French that made her not like him as much—he used the same voice as the police and the impatient aid workers. When they reached the mouth of the huge tent he gave her arm a quick squeeze.

"You'll be safe here," he said, his voice now softer and familiar. But she hesitated, and the other girls stared at the European doctor in their midst. "Dépêche-toi," he said sharply, *hurry up.* Lalande didn't look back at her over his shoulder as he left.

Adah found a patch of tarped ground unoccupied and lowered herself between an albino, who couldn't have been more than ten and was crying softly in her sleep, and a girl closer to her own age whose eyes were open crescents of moonlight staring at nothing. Her dark skin and large breasts reminded Adah of her own mother, known only by the sacred photograph, long dead in her stony grave in the desert, bones surely white and polished, shining somewhere wordlessly. Complicit in a comfort that would hearten them for a moment, that would feel like love although they both knew it was only warmth, the two girls embraced the animal warmth of keening flesh pressed to keening flesh. Adah's lips found the girl's earlobe, and her tongue that would not speak sucked the salt from the girl's skin, sustaining her and keeping her alive for the night. They slept like that, without language and almost content.

Adah heard the fire before she smelled it, the yawning, whistle-pop of grass burning at the edge of the enclosure — surely a careless candle or cigarette coal had dropped, and it was creeping now, orange fingers teasing and caressing the side of the canvas tarp, licking upwards toward the black sky. The girl slept, and Adah wanted to touch her, wake her, but the girl would scream and then there would be bodies flailing everywhere. There would be people trampled and afterward someone to blame. There would be talk and questions she could not speak to answer and she would be ensnared. By the time Adah heard the first shouts about the fire, she was already fifty yards away. She hoped the girl would wake up soon, if she hadn't already. It was always safer to go alone.

Adah sat on the little hill where the medic tent was and drew her legs to her chest. The smoke rolled and billowed from the burning tents all across the camp, not just the Girl's Camp where she had slept. The sun was coming up and Adah saw that several large mobile-response-unit vehicles had driven into the Jungle. It was the police who were setting the fires, and who were rounding people up into busses; they meant to clear the camp. She heard the shuffle-hop of Matteau as he approached her from behind—by now she could recognize his walk even over the din of the camp being dismantled—and he laboriously sat next to her, wrapping his arm around her shoulders. He wore a black hoodie like the one she wore, and she imagined that from a distance they must look like two hunched birds with dark wings.

"This means you're getting out," he said. She shook her head at him and pressed her body closer to his. *It means we're getting out*, Adah thought.

"No," Matteau said, reading her mind. "The doctor will take you. He came here looking for someone to save. No one is coming for me." This was her punishment for caring for Matteau, Adah knew, to see him stay behind. If only Adah could bring Matteau out, too. But he could never catch a train or sneak onto a lorry or pass for what he was not. She gave him the last Dunhill and they sat and smoked it together. It tasted terrible, like burning flesh. The little white trails from the cigarette rose up and added themselves to the growing cloud of smoke that moved across the sky from the burning camp. The fires were erasing the Jungle, Adah thought. She took the cross necklace from Aunt Maia off and pressed it into Matteau's hand. He looked at her strangely.

"Friend," he said, "You should know I believe in nothing." Adah folded his hand over the little carved cross, a talisman of everything that was meaningless but hopeful in the world. She wanted to tell Matteau that he would make it, she wanted to tell him she would find him on the other side, in England. But Adah knew that even if she were capable of saying the words they would be false promises that would die in the air between them and be carried off with the smoke that was the camp disappearing into the sky.

When Adah came to the medic tent the sulfur stink of burning shelters and garbage was thick. Lalande was packing his cases of medical instruments and bottles of peroxide and rolls of white gauze into plastic bins. He failed to see Adah at first, moving past her as all the others did, until she finally flung her voice at him, making him turn, his Dunhill with its long ash hanging from his lips. He grabbed her with such force she thought he meant to throw her back out of the tent, but instead he shoved her into a wheelchair and wrapped a shawl over her head.

"Today we leave," he said. "It's over. They are closing down the Jungle for good." He nodded at her until she mirrored him, bobbing her head along with him, and there was something in his green eyes that Adah recognized from the way boys looked at girls in her old village—he meant to keep her for himself.

With the camp closing, there was confusion everywhere. Adah kept her eyes down as Lalande wheeled her past the line of police holding large guns and wearing helmets with plastic shields, then into the back of a dented white van. It didn't look like any official vehicle Adah had seen, and Adah realized that it must belong to Lalande himself, rather than to Médecins Sans Frontières. Lalande secured the wheelchair to the floor of the vehicle with a steel cable and put a surgical mask on her face and locked the doors of the van.

"They must believe you are very sick. Understand?" said Lalande. Adah nodded, and Lalande drove towards the barricades. Adah closed her eyes and felt the clank of the metal wheelchair against the floor in her bones as they bumped to a stop. When she heard the window roll down, she listened to Lalande speak in an impatient, angular French with the guard. She could not understand the language, but the voice of the officer was unyielding and she felt she might lose consciousness. The exhaust inside the van was making her nauseous, and she tried to hold her breath, but she finally lurched forward in the chair, voiding the water and rice in her stomach onto the van floor. The argument between the two men stopped and Adah flopped back in the wheelchair.

"Allons-y," said the guard, "C'est l'heure!" He waved them through, spitting onto the ground before pulling his helmet's visor back down over his face.

LALANDE'S APARTMENT WAS NEAR the railyard and the docks that they had passed as they drove away from the camp. The air was heavy and damp, and Lalande seemed nervous as he unclipped the wheelchair from the floor of the transport van. He didn't speak or look at Adah's face as he walked her up the narrow stairs to his apartment, and she wondered what he had risked or lost by taking her from the camp and into what must have been, for him at least, the real world.

The door shut behind them, and Adah was surprised to see how empty the apartment was—she had thought a doctor would have more. A row of his identical indigo shirts hung on hooks by the door. The kitchen was attached to the living room, which contained only a desk, a battered green sofa, a few chairs, a scarred table with a candle on it and a single shelf nailed to the wall that was filled with *National Geographic* magazines, their yellow spines combining to make one long, golden bar.

"You must be hungry?" Lalande said, his voice unsure. So full of authority at the camp, he now seemed frightened, as if he had made some great mistake by bringing her here. Lalande brought Adah a slab of cheese and a hunk of bread from the kitchenette. He watched her intently as she ate, and then he produced a glass of orange juice for her. It tasted like liquid sunlight. He opened a new pack of cigarettes and began to smoke them by the window in succession. Now that they were outside of the camp, nothing seemed normal.

They sat on the sofa together, and Lalande lit the candle in its brass candlestick and placed it on the table. He took a magazine from the shelf. In the unsteady candlelight, he folded the page back, creasing it with his tobacco-stained thumbnail, carving the ink from the illustrations on the page. His short nails were ridged and divided with vertical lines, as though they had been hammered from a thin sheet of metal. Adah had the idea that she would like to research the patterns of his body, to discover the secret of him at the first chance she got. Lalande began to read:

During the Pleistocene epoch Earth was populated with mega-fauna. Many huge mammals resembled their contemporary counter-

parts, but weighed over 1,000 kilograms. Around 11,700 years ago
at the end of the last Ice Age, thousands of species died out as early
humans began spreading across the Earth, leading some scientists to
believe that human predation, rather than disease or climate change,
could have been the cause of these extinctions.

The animals marched along the timeline in the magazine
in ever decreasing numbers: a wild, mythic heard of wool-
ly mammoths, saber-toothed tigers, and, most interesting to
Adah, giant tapirs—creatures with the graceful musculature of
a large antelope but the tusked face of a wild boar and striped
flanks like a zebra. They towered over a little man in a loin-
cloth with a thick forehead and a spear clutched in his tiny fist.
Lalande tapped each animal's illustration, saying their names
like a chant: Mammoth. Tiger. Giant Tapir. How could these
magnificent beasts succumb to something as inferior as this
scraggly, reaching man, Adah wondered. How could the giant
tapir, with its brilliant stripes and perfect teeth and quivering
flanks fail to survive because of men? If Adah herself had been
of that animal's tribe, she would have made sure of her surviv-
al, she thought. If there were no more plants, she would have
switched to meat. If she were hunted, she would have found
a way to make humans her food instead. She leaned closer
to where Lalande reclined on the sofa and began undoing the

buttons on his shirt. Adah smoothed her hands across Lalande's concave belly. She rolled her fingertips over his smooth, sunken stomach, discovering that he had almost no navel to speak of. He looked at her with something like despair and went into his bedroom, shutting the door behind him. He emerged a few minutes later with a folded gray wool blanket and a pillow.

"You'll sleep here, until we can decide where you are going," he said. After he left, Adah could hear him speaking in French on the phone in a hurried voice, and because she could understand nothing that was being said, she found that it all sounded like a plot to contain her, to keep her in France and away from the life that she could have had in England. Lalande would eventually decide she should be transferred to an agency, Adah thought, and he was not really equipped to take her anywhere with him. The two of them were not of the same kind.

Once she was convinced that Lalande was asleep, Adah went to the kitchen and drank a second glass of orange juice. She found a pair of scissors in a drawer and clipped the picture of the giant tapir from the magazine, leaving the little caveman behind. Adah pressed the image of the animal flat inside the Bible next to the picture of her mother. She took one of Lalande's indigo shirts from the hooks by the door and put it on underneath her black sweatshirt. The cotton fabric was crisp against her skin. She walked out of the apartment, and the latch clicked behind her as she shut the door. For a moment Adah was sorry that she didn't leave a note, and she wondered if Lalande would be disappointed that he had chosen the wrong person to save.

Adah followed the road away from Lalande's apartment toward the sea. She could smell the port, the slick salt scent and gritty metal tang in her nose. As she got closer they were everywhere, migrants like her, moving like shadows, the charred smell of the camp still wafting off them. No one spoke or gave directions, but she could find the place easily; they were all going that way. Some pulled suitcases, but many, like Adah, carried nothing.

After a time, she saw the railyard and the port ahead, and someone was helping people through a hole cut in a chain-link fence. She moved toward it silently, and there was Jahid, holding the steel mesh to the side for her as she passed through. He would not be defeated, and Adah had always known that about him, so perhaps it should not surprise her to see him here, so near to the crossing point. His eyes registered her, and Adah knew he saw it in her, too, that ability to withstand, to survive. "Ib'd," he said, *go away*. He raised his free hand, as if in benediction, to wave her through. Adah followed the tracks with the others towards the arch of the tunnel, open like a dark mouth of cement and steel. Adah heard the pounding of an approaching train, though it was still miles away. The tracks were choked with them now, hundreds marching toward the crush of traffic and police running past them in the chaos, for once not bothering to try to push the migrants into straight lines. The time to cross was coming soon. Adah knew she would not fall, because she belonged to no one but herself and there was nobody left to catch her. She knew she would grip tightly and press close to the train's oiled heaving mass, and her hands sang with the knowledge that they would carry her through the darkness and that she would be reborn on the other side, where the entire world beckoned and waited to receive her. England, where the streets trembled and shook with light.

ACKNOWLEDGMENTS

My thanks:

To the students, faculty, and staff of the low-residency MFA in Writing Program at Spalding University, for creating what is truly a vibrant creative community and a home for writers. To Robin Lippincott, dear friend and mentor extraordinaire. To Helena Kriel and to Leslie Daniels, for their belief in my writing and for their friendship.

To the Fleur-de-Lis publishing team, especially Ellyn Lichvar and Jonathan Weinert, for their dedicated work on this publication. To Matthew Walsh for his unparalleled cover artwork.

To all the dear friends, readers, editors, and colleagues who have supported me in every possible way, especially Julie Brickman, Roy Burkhead, Charles Entrekin, Roy Hoffman, Sarah Houston, Nancy Jensen, Karen Mann, the late Julia Mature, Nancy Brooks Moore, Eleanor Morse, Bonnie

Omer Johnson, Elaine Orr, Frederick Smock, Lucinda Dixon Sullivan, Neela Vaswani, and Mary Yukari Waters.

To my family, including my father, Alan Naslund, my uncles, Marvin D. Jeter and John Sims Jeter, Nona Burns Schildknecht, and Judith Ford.

To my treasured sister Andra, for her ongoing love and encouragement.

To Ron, my beloved husband, for his kind heart and limitless enthusiasm for our creative endeavors, who has nurtured me and my writing at every turn.

To my mother, Sena Jeter Naslund, who has inspired so many to find fulfillment, joy, and success both in writing and in life, and whose championing of these stories made this collection possible.

ABOUT THE AUTHOR

Kylene White

Flora K. Schildknecht has published fiction in *The Louisville Review*, *2nd & Church*, *The Chaffin Journal*, and *Sisyphus*. Her work has been nominated twice for the Pushcart prize. She earned an MFA from Spalding University, where she studied fiction and screenwriting. Her love of travel has taken her to Japan, Tanzania, Argentina, Mexico, Great Britain, and to Scandinavia and much of Europe. She lives with her husband and their son in Louisville, Kentucky, and teaches at Bellarmine University. She and her family often enjoy weekends at their condo in the Lakeview East neighborhood of Chicago.

Fleur-de-Lis Press is named to celebrate the life

of Flora Lee Sims Jeter

(1901–1990)